It May Not Leave a Scar

Also by Milam Propst

A Flower Blooms on Charlotte Street

IT MAY NOT LEAVE A SCAR

A Novel

by

MILAM MCGRAW PROPST

Mercer
University
Press
2001

ISBN 0-86554-719-X
MUP/H539

© 2001 Mercer University Press
6316 Peake Road
Macon, Georgia 31210-3960
All rights reserved

First Edition.

∞The paper used in this publication meets the minimum
requirements of American National Standard for Information
Sciences—Permanence of Paper for Printed Library Materials, ANSI
Z39.48-1992.

CIP information is on file with the Library of Congress

I dedicate this book to my mother, Mary Catherine Whitman McGraw, who introduced me to her faith and provided the circumstances for me to find my own strength through it.

Acknowledgments

With my love to James Edward Propst, Jr., my husband and sweet Daddy to our grown children. Resourceful man that he has always been, just yesterday steadied my steering wheel so that I, balancing pen, paper, and a cell phone, could take notes from one of my editors, Kevin Manus. Thanks to Jamey for his ongoing efforts to keep me safely on the road all throughout our marriage.

With gratitude to precious friends, wishing I could mention each and everyone who has carried me over the bumps of being me. This novel brings to mind a few women whom I must single out: to Pam Weeks for her willingness to hear each new chapter as I wrote and rewrote this novel; to Betty Ann Colley for four decades of friendship and shared faith, to Jackie Brown and Betty George for their years of "prayers to publish," and to Jaclyn White, my indomitable book-signing buddy and marketing mentor.

To those who encourage: Mary and Marvin Brantley, Ave Bransford, the Carrolls, the O'Connors, the Davis Family, Cornelia Jolly, Valiere Kuffrey, Ruth Maquire, "all Dem Walthers," Georganne Donnelly, Ociee A. Robnett, and Marilynn Winston, Ph.D.

And to the incredible artists group, Beverly Key, Dorothy Brooks, Lalor Ferarri, Janet Hagerman, and Janet Wells.

And, as always, to the talented woman who will forever remain my teacher, Sister Thomas Margaret. About STM I must declare, "She's not 'the same old 76,' either."

With devotion to the Propst children, our sons William and Jay, and to the girls who love them, Abigail and Christa. To our daughter Amanda, much of what is inside and outside of this book is from her.

Special thanks are also due my hero, Marc Jolley, Ph. D., assistant publisher at Mercer University Press; to Kevin Manus, the manuscript editor who pulled me kicking and screaming to the end of this journey, and to the other hard-working and supportive people at Mercer University Press, who nourish my creative endeavors and share the victories that have been awarded to our first effort together, *A Flower Blooms on Charlotte Street.*

Lastly and most importantly, I place the acceptance of *It May Not Leave a Scar* in the hands of God, my Father in heaven. I offer my sincere appreciation to Him for all the kind and caring people that He has placed along my path and for the words He has put in my heart to speak.

Milam McGraw Propst
December 24, 2000

1

A single shot. A thud. Then there was quiet. No movement. Only an eerie stillness consumed the Sinclair family's home. No voice broke the uncanny silence that engulfed it. No bird's song drifted in through the windows. No breeze disturbed the trees or rustled summer's soft green leaves. No automobile motored its way down Harbert Street.

Her heart pounding, Sarah Sinclair ran stumbling up the steps of the mahogany spiral staircase. She screamed with every step, yet no sound escaped her mouth. Sarah's chest was heaving as she reached the top of the stairs. Throwing open the master bedroom door, Sarah found the lifeless body of her husband.

"Eugene!" she shrieked.

Sarah collapsed atop him and wailed. The carnage from the gun's blast dripped down the beveled mirror door of the wardrobe. Like deep, dark crimson paint, Eugene Sinclair's fresh blood soaked into the royal blue, gold, and rich cream colors of the oriental carpet. As Sarah wept passionately, her tears intermingled with the growing stain in her husband's dressing gown.

Imogene Sinclair turned into the driveway. The petite, blue-eyed, eighteen-year-old college girl, with her newly-coifed blond waves bouncing, glanced in the rearview mirror and grinned at the excitement of being behind the wheel of her mother's green roadster.

The Connors pulled into their drive next door just as Imogene was walking up the path. Mr. Connor got out of his car and waved at her. "How's your father feeling today? My wife's been praying for him every night."

"Thank you, Mr. Connor. I don't know. I left for class before Mother woke him this morning," answered Imogene. "But she did say Daddy seemed a little perkier last night."

She slung her handbag over her shoulder and bounded onto the front porch. The afternoon had been a pleasant one for a change. Ever since her father's automobile accident, not too many days had felt quite as hopeful to her.

Pulling shut the heavy front door, Imogene announced, "Mother, I'm home." She walked in the direction of the study. "How's Daddy? Is he any better this afternoon?"

No answer.

"Mother?"

Imogene turned her head to listen for a reply. Nothing. Only Sarah's opened book lying on the study floor gave evidence she'd been reading. Imogene heard an odd noise coming from another part of the house.

"Mother?"

Still there was no response. She returned to the foyer and listened more intently. Again she heard the strange sound, a sound of moaning, coming from the second floor.

"Daddy!" In panic, she raced straight up to her parents' room.

"Mother! No!" Imogene screamed as she froze in place.

Sarah clutched Eugene's gun in her right hand. She had it pointed at her chest.

Click. Sarah pulled the trigger. *Click, click, click, click.* Sarah hurled the empty gun across the room and sank down on the bed.

Slowly, Imogene's head turned toward the crumpled figure on the floor.

"*Daddy*!" Imogene let out an inhuman shriek that shook the walls of the Sinclair house.

Hearing the scream, the Connors let themselves in through the kitchen door and hurried up the back staircase. Mrs. Connor steadied herself, clutching tightly to her husband's arm.

The bloodied wardrobe greeted the couple as they entered the bedroom.

"Good God, what happened here?" shouted Mr. Connor.

"Sarah?" cried his wife. "Imogene? Eugene!"

Sarah stood up, trembling, and paced about the large room, twisting her fingers, muttering. As the Connors looked on, she turned quickly and approached Imogene. She whispered her daughter's name, "Imogene." Sarah reached out toward her daughter, but just as quickly, she hesitated and drew back her extended hand. She curled her arms close to her neck.

Mrs. Connor went to Sarah's side, "Now, now, my dear Sarah, let's go into another room, shall we?" The kind neighbor motioned for Imogene to follow them. Imogene simply stared. Her mouth hung open. Tears streamed down her cheeks.

Mr. Connor went downstairs to telephone Doctor Johnson.

Imogene dropped to her knees beside her cherished Daddy and began to inspect his strangely alien face, touching it gently.

Imogene gagged. Then she threw up on Eugene's blood-soaked form. Seemingly unaware of the vomit that covered her front, the young girl began to cry out to her mother and to the Connors, "Get help. Hurry, get help!" Imogene gripped her father's hand. With her free hand, she gestured wildly and shouted, "Go! Hurry, get the doctor!"

Sarah stared off into space, unresponsive.

"Imogene, darling, it's too late," repeated Mrs. Connor over and over again.

"It is not. *Daddy is alive*," she pleaded. "Please call for someone to come."

Mr. Connor returned shortly, announcing, "Dr. Johnson is on his way."

Imogene smiled as she clung to Eugene's limp hand. "Thank you, Mr. Connor." She added, "See, Daddy, you're going to be all right."

Mrs. Connor replied, "Please, my dear, no one can do anything for your darling father now."

Imogene didn't reply.

By the time Dr. Johnson arrived, other neighbors and family had filtered into the house. One woman encouraged Sarah to drink a sip of water. She agreed, but putting the glass to her lips, she choked. Even water couldn't find its way down the woman's grief-constricted throat.

Tom Johnson, M.D., had been in the medical field for more than twenty years. Even so, when the physician saw the shattered head of his lifelong friend, he could only gasp. There would be no miracle this day.

Dr. Johnson examined Eugene and made the necessary notations in his records. His pen hovered above the paper before writing the word "suicide."

Swallowing his own grief, the doctor picked Eugene up into his arms and carried him across the room. He carefully laid the body in the four-poster bed that Eugene had shared with Sarah.

The physician moved quickly about the bedroom trying to conceal the horror of Eugene's suicide. He wrapped Eugene's head in a towel and covered his friend's body with the heavy damask bedspread. Then, having done all he could think to do,

Tom Johnson buried his face in his hands, breathed deeply, and prayed.

White as a sheet and still trembling, Sarah rocked back and forth in the sunroom. Two ladies from the neighborhood sat on either side of her. They rose quickly making a place for the doctor as he entered.

"I am so sorry, Sarah," Tom uttered.

"I never would have dreamed—" Her words broke mid-sentence. "Oh, Tom, what about Imogene?"

"Your brother-in-law is with her now. I'll check on her in just a minute," he assured her. "Let me give you a sedative, something to calm you."

"Tom, no! I must, I must do...I must do *something*. Tom, what is it that I must do?" Sarah pleaded.

"Just rest. There is little else that anyone can do at this moment," replied the physician as he gave her an injection. "Please, just lie back. Try to rest. Sarah, you'll have many people who will be with you to see you through this."

Sarah closed her eyes, weeping softly, and finally drifted off into a fitful sleep.

Despite the pleas of her neighbors and family, Imogene stood in the doorway of her parents' bedroom. The scene in the bedroom was oddly familiar to Imogene, not unlike the way the room had looked to her throughout the last three weeks. The draperies were drawn. The marble dresser was cluttered with medicine, and close by on a side table was a tray of untouched food. Eugene's clean pajamas were folded on the upholstered chair by the window. His glasses were still positioned on top of some reading materials, and there were vases of flowers from well-wishers along with bowls of uneaten fruit.

What was different was her father's utter stillness. There he lay beneath a bedspread—only sleeping, perhaps? No, he wasn't sleeping. Missing was the rise and fall of her father's chest.

Eugene's eyes were shut. His mouth was flat and emotionless. Her father's full, rosy cheeks were sunken in and chalk white. His smiling face had been transformed into that of a gargoyle.

"No!" Imogene yelled. She turned and bolted from the room. Imogene charged down the staircase. She stopped midway. A swelling sea of faces at the foot of the stairs turned to meet her. She announced loudly to those faces, "I'm getting the hell out of here!"

More heads turned as mouths dropped open. Someone commented, "That's the daughter, isn't it?"

Hearing the question, Imogene roared, "*It* is. *It* is the *daughter*." She frowned and, eyes wide, searched feverishly for her purse.

Hearing the commotion, Dr. Johnson left the slumbering Sarah and hurried to stop Imogene from leaving. "Imogene! Wait dear, stop, please!"

A neighbor ran across the dining room and reached out quickly grabbing the hysterical young woman's shoulder. "Wait a moment, child," she cautioned. "Please, try to get a hold of yourself!"

"Get a hold of *yourself*," Imogene responded. "I need a cigarette." She tore herself free from the lady's grasp.

"Well, I'll be...," the neighbor began.

Dr. Johnson put his finger to his lips to silence her. He nodded and patted the woman's back as if to explain away Imogene's angry reaction.

The car door slammed as Imogene hurled herself into the front seat. She got into her mother's car and drove around Forest Park until the car ran out of gas.

It rained all night after the funeral and into the next day. In the weeks to come, Sarah abandoned her stylish clothes. She gave away most of her finer things and chose to dress in a simple housecoat. On the rare days she ventured out from the Sinclair home, she wore the same plain, black suit.

Her diamond bracelet, the cameos, the dinner ring she had always worn when out for an evening, her wedding ring, all the treasures so carefully chosen by Eugene were pitched into a shoe box and hidden away in the back of her dressing table drawer.

She took no calls and ate only sparingly. Most of her time was spent in the master bedroom with the door shut, but never again did Sarah sleep in their bed.

It was a month or more before the young widow allowed her husband's bloodstains to be removed from the oriental rug. The cleaning of it signaled one less bond with Eugene.

In August, Sarah sold their bed. She sobbed as the van carrying it turned the corner at the end of the street.

Imogene did not seem to notice the changes in her mother. She exchanged her days for the cover of night. She left the house every afternoon and headed out in any direction she felt like, not returning until the small hours of the morning.

Imogene decided to change her name. She suddenly thought "Imogene" too childish, reverting instead to her high school nickname of "Mo."

She raced Sarah's car around the streets and boulevards of Memphis and throughout the surrounding countryside as well. Mo's second trademark, a cigarette, dangled from her lips. She also began to carry her father's silver flask engraved with his initials, "E. W. S." At first filled with water, it soon contained some kind of alcohol she pilfered from her father's liquor cabinet.

One evening, Imogene wheeled into her friend Gina's driveway and honked the horn. Gina ran outside to greet her friend. "Imogene, what are you doing here?"

"It's *Mo*, Gina. Come on, let's go for a little ride."

"Oh, no, you know I can't," she replied. "Mother would worry."

Imogene was close enough to see her friend's wink. That was their signal. So she drove around the block and waited. Within ten minutes, Gina appeared. She jumped in the car and off they went.

"Do you think she knew you sneaked out?" asked Mo.

"Probably, but Mother's just worn out from arguing with me about everything. You know she really doesn't approve of us being together so much either."

"Looks like I've become a bad influence," laughed Mo as she presented the flask.

"And?" said Gina.

"Go on, smell what's in it, my dear," answered Mo.

"My God, is it whiskey?"

"Yep, I stole it from home."

"Good grief, Mo, you are the bad girl!"

"Maybe so. Hey, let's get some Coca-Cola. Stuff's pretty strong by itself," Mo suggested.

The giggling girls made their way to downtown Memphis, parked the car, and took a walk by the Mississippi. Finding a good spot, obscured from sight by some big trees, they mixed the bourbon with Coke in paper cups. The old friends talked and drank.

"I will if you will," Mo said, nodding toward the river and unbuttoning her dress.

"I don't think so," laughed Gina as she shook her head.

"C'mon!" shouted Mo jumping up and stripping off her dress. She got down to her brassiere and panties and raced down toward the Mississippi.

"You're a crazy fool, Imogene!" yelled Gina. "You're gonna drown, girl!" But their drinks had dimmed their good sense. Soon Gina, too, wearing only her underwear, was splashing about in the river.

They paddled around in the cool river's water as the moonlight danced like tiny stars circling them. Out in the river, a barge chugged by making waves that jostled the laughing girls. Lights of the city sparkled like Christmas trees in the night sky.

"Isn't this the greatest feeling!" squealed Mo.

"Hell, yes!" Gina screamed.

"Race ya' across?" Mo challenged.

"Let me get some fuel first," said Gina, heading toward the river bank.

"Bring me another drink, too," Mo shouted after her friend.

As Gina poured the drinks, lights flashed up on the bluff.

"What's going on down here?" demanded an unusually large and commanding officer.

As the officer made his way toward them, Gina hastily threw on her clothes and tossed the flask under the car. As the officer drew near, Gina pointed out toward the river and responded breathlessly, "Thank goodness you're here! My friend has fallen into the river!"

The policeman aimed his light out into the water.

Mo saw him. "Where's the fire?" she slurred.

"Young lady, are you all right?" he called.

"'Course, I am, Mr. Fireman," said Mo, paddling leisurely toward the bank.

A second policeman offered a blanket to Gina who, out of total fear of being taken into custody, had quickly hidden her own intoxication.

Offering Mo his hand as she clambered out of the water, the larger officer said, "What do you think you're doing, Miss? Are you trying to kill yourself?"

"Could be," Mo jeered. "Seems to run in my family."

Gina had hurried to her friend's side with a second blanket. "I'll take her home, officer. She'll be fine. She's just been through a bad ordeal with her family."

"Well, I'm sorry about that, little lady." He hesitated. "I suppose, if you agree to drive her, it should be all right."

Mo piped up, "Drive me! Gina can't drive, Mr. Fireman."

"Of course, I can, Mo. I'm older than you," she said winking at the officer. "She's been so upset, you see."

The officer looked at the two young women. "I suppose I could let this go for now, but you *both* go straight home and get to bed before you get hurt. No more of these shenanigans in the river! It's very dangerous out there, you hear me?"

"Yes, sir," said Gina speaking for the two of them. As soon as the policeman was out of sight, Gina retrieved the flask. They got into Sarah's car. Gina said, "Now, how in the heck do I drive this thing?"

"There's nothing to it!" answered Mo as she unscrewed the flask and took a sip, a sip without the soft drink to cut the sting. Gina shoved the gearshift into place and jerking her foot off the clutch, she stomped the gas. The car lunged forward.

Unusually beautiful, the frenzied young lady accepted the invitations of nearly every suitor who asked her for a date. And should the young man not have arranged dinner plans, Mo would dine on potato chips, Cokes, and ice cream sundaes.

Sarah spent her waking hours wandering the silent Sinclair home and awaiting Imogene's return. She worried about her daughter well into the wee hours after midnight and often stood at the window watching the street.

Eventually Mo would wander in and go back to the kitchen to pour herself a glass of milk. As soon as the front door slammed shut, Sarah breathed a sigh of relief. After downing the milk, Mo went to her room and collapsed into slumber.

Neither woman ever uttered a word.

Certain her daughter was soundly asleep, Sarah crept into Imogene's bedroom and covered her with a soft blue blanket. She'd stand at the foot of her bed watching her daughter sleep. Her own sleep could finally come as she curled her ever thinning body into a knot on the divan in the sunroom.

On a crisp, unseasonably cool evening in mid-September, Imogene had gone to a football game with a group of young men and women. Upon returning home, she crawled upstairs to the bathroom where she vomited in the sink. Drunk and disoriented, Mo spun around and, again missing the toilet, threw up in the bathtub.

Sarah woke from a fitful sleep downstairs and tapped on the bathroom door. "Imogene? Dear? Are you okay?"

Imogene gagged again.

Sarah pounded on the door until Mo opened it. She covered her mouth with her hand when she saw her daughter.

Mo's wet hair was stuck to her face. Her blue eyes were rimmed in blood red. Her mouth hung open. Vomit covered her white cotton blouse. "Mus' have eaten some bad shrimp," she slurred.

Sarah's stomach tightened as she surveyed the bathroom. It was all she could do to keep down the small amount of dinner she'd forced herself to eat. Swallowing down the bile that rose in her throat, she said, "Just go to bed. I'll take care of this."

Mo staggered past her. Bumping her hip on a table, she fell crossways onto the bed. Sarah scrubbed the bathroom with bleach. An hour later, she applied lotion to her hands that were red and raw from the sickening task. That night the mother didn't go into her daughter's room.

The next morning, the new widow purposefully threw open the draperies in the parlor, raised the window and took a deep breath. Steadying herself on the back of a chair, she proclaimed, "The leaves will soon be changing, Sarah Sinclair. It's time you made some changes for yourself."

A week later, she bought two one-way tickets to New Orleans. She announced to her daughter that they would be going to visit her family there.

"Why not? I'm bored anyway," said Mo.

Sarah made arrangements to sell her car and close up the house. Without sharing her decision with many people beyond Will (Eugene's brother), the neighbors, and Dr. Johnson, she quietly packed enough items and clothes necessary for an undetermined length of time.

She yearned to escape the gossip surrounding Eugene's suicide and the well-meant, though endless, remarks of sympathy. Sarah was tired of being regarded as a "poor thing." She sought sanctuary with her Aunt Hattie on the outskirts of New Orleans, in a place called Metarie.

2

Aunt Hattie proved to be all Sarah had hoped she'd be. A rail-thin, gregarious spinster whose gold rimmed eyeglasses balanced precisely on the tip of her nose, Hattie knew every neighbor for blocks around her Metarie neighborhood. "What good will it do any of us to dwell on what cannot be undone?" Hattie encouraged.

A month or so after she and Imogene arrived, Hattie introduced them to a gentleman named Mr. Jones who had a well-established law practice in downtown New Orleans. Hattie realized that Mo had too much time on her hands and she hoped to get the young woman interested in some type of work.

Following the conversation about a possible job for Imogene, Sarah retreated to the warm autumn sunshine of Hattie's back porch. Her aunt walked out into the flower garden. "We should have a good many more blooms to enjoy before the chill comes," Aunt Hattie announced. Sarah smiled back, but her mind was on her own first job years ago.

Before the words could stick in the throat, Sarah called out to her aunt, "Hattie, do you suppose I could apply for Mr. Jones's job?"

Her aunt was taken aback. "You, Sarah? Why, I had no idea!" said her aunt. She put down her basket of flowers and hurried up onto the porch.

"Aunt Hattie, even beyond trying to go on with my life without my darling Eugene," she sighed, "Imogene and I are also having to live without his income."

"Of course, poor dears, if you need anything, anything at all," began Hattie.

"No, Aunt Hattie, certainly not! You've done much too much already. I just believe that if I could get that position with the lawyer, I could stand on my own. What do you think? Will your Mr. Jones give me a chance? I've held positions before, of course," she said. "We, Eugene and I, met at my office," she finished faintly.

"Yes, dear, of course, I remember," said Hattie.

"Hattie, it's also Imogene that concerns me. My daughter needs to find something to occupy her time. She is so young," her voice trailed off.

"Indeed, she is. I thought she might enjoy working downtown," offered Hattie.

"Well, the fact is that one of us must find a way to earn an income, and I am the one who has had the experience. And the maturity! I feel it is my responsibility."

Hattie smiled as she listened.

"I was very efficient, too, as I recall," she said. "Oh, Hattie, that was so awfully long ago, wasn't it?" she added with a groan.

"Dear Sarah," said Hattie, patting Sarah's hand, "you have always been smart. Even as a little girl you were quite quick to catch on with your studies. Mr. Jones needs someone, and he trusts my judgment. Consider yourself employed."

After only a few months had passed, Sarah, Hattie, and Mr. Jones knew she'd made the right decision. Sarah Sinclair enjoyed her work and learned quickly. She managed to find a suitable apartment closer to work and wrote to her brother-in-law asking him to sell their Memphis home for her.

Mo, on the contrary, couldn't have worried less about income or jobs or anything else. She had fallen easily into the same patterns that she had during her turbulent last few weeks in Memphis.

Mo accrued a curious array of new friends, all of whom frequented the notorious nightspots of the French Quarter. She celebrated with the wildest of the revelers at the costume balls during Mardi Gras. The week leading up to Lent was to become her most favorite time of the year. The young woman discovered a quirky kind of identity as she donned a variety of intriguing disguises for the balls.

One evening, while awaiting the arrival of her date to the ball, Mo checked her harlequin costume, purple and gold, in the hall mirror. Touching her mask, she said, "Perfect."

Soon there was a knock at the door and George, her date, escorted her to the car. He opened the door and she jumped in. Before he could get settled in the driver's seat, Mo was leaning toward him with Eugene's flask in hand. "A little something for the road?" She winked.

"Oh, no thanks," he said, "I'm not much of a drinker."

"Suit yourself," she answered as she turned up the flask. "This just might do you some good, you know. Builds confidence."

"Is that a fact?" he responded.

This is going to be one long evening, thought Imogene as she adjusted her mask. "So, who are you supposed to be?"

"I'm Merlin," he said. "You remember, Merlin the Magician from the court of King Arthur. I like your outfit; a harlequin I see. We are a good pair for a royal court: a harlequin and a wizard! We're just what any well-rounded king would require." He laughed nervously.

"And I need another little sippy," she said.

By the time they arrived, Mo was ready to dance. She quickly jilted George for a tall blond knight. After they had their first couple of dances, the knight suggested they get some air out on the veranda of the ballroom. As soon as they got outside, he tried to kiss Mo. As he touched her mask, she slapped him.

"I'm sorry," he pleaded. "I just thought...well."

"Well what?" she snapped at him. She turned on her heel and returned to the ball.

George saw her coming. He brightened up. She saw him and spun around in the opposite direction. It didn't take Mo long to find another man with whom to dance. "I have one rule," she said to her new partner. "No one is allowed to touch my mask."

In the winter of 1934, Mo married Harvey Clark. She had met the curly-haired young salesman from Baton Rouge in a French Quarter bar. Six weeks later, they took a 3:00 A.M. trolley ride to the office of a justice of the peace. Wobbling before the sleepy man, Mo and Harvey laughed their way through a wedding ceremony. No one, not even Sarah or Aunt Hattie, knew about it until the next morning.

Mo became Sarah Imogene Sinclair *Clark*. From the very first time she said her new name out loud her new last name sounded to the new bride like a mistake at the end of a too long sentence.

Sarah saw Harvey as a young man intent on his work and most assuredly head over heels in love with her daughter. Initially disappointed with their elopement, Sarah finally convinced herself it was a *practical* thing to do. After all, he must have realized that financial issues were to be considered when trying to plan a wedding. Sarah only hoped Harvey would be as half as devoted to Imogene as had been her father.

"At least Mother likes Harvey. Now that's a point in the poor guy's favor." She took a puff. "Besides, I won't have to try work anymore." She thought of her dreary job as a sales clerk in the dreadful little dress shop. "I'll have more time to play bridge."

Harvey was ambitious. An amiable traveling salesman for a large industrial company, he wanted to get ahead which meant travel. His new bride played bridge. The more Harvey traveled, the more Mo played bridge. And the more bridge Mo played, the more afternoon toddies she drank with the bridge gals. Finally, the group and Harvey's wife abandoned the cards all together.

The girls met at Mo and Harvey's apartment one morning just after ten in the morning. Mo had had a few drinks that night before and had struggled to get up early enough to go to the French Market for some freshly-baked powdered sugar donuts. She had to return quickly, no time to enjoy her breakfast, and hurriedly readied the apartment for her three guests. She gulped down some more orange juice, emptied the trash and pushed the dust mop around the couple's small living room.

"That will have to do," she said as she started the thick chicory coffee. Its strong scent masked the heavy layer of stale cigarettes that hung in the air of the tiny downtown apartment.

Mo winced at the bright morning sun filtering through the windows. She poured more juice as she waited for the coffee to perk.

A few cups of coffee later, the apartment was full.

"I'll open with three hearts," said Kathryn.

"Three no trump," bid her partner.

The donuts were soon gone, and Mo brought out some maple sugar pralines she had purchased the day before.

"Lord have mercy, girl," said Polly, "What are you trying to do to us? Make us fat?!"

Mo laughed. "No, you know I hate to cook, and with Harvey always gone, I can eat anything I damn well please. I'm partial to goodies like this. Have one."

"Mo Clark, are you pregnant?" Polly suddenly inquired.

"Heavens no! What? Oh, I'll pass again, I'm just not getting any good hands today. Polly, what would I do with a baby?" She added, "It's all I can do to take care of this place and, as you can see, to try to learn how to bid properly."

By mid-afternoon, the coffee had long been replaced with Coca-Cola or iced tea. Before long, Mo was adding her own dash of flavor to her Coke. In the kitchen as she poured in some vodka, she confided to Polly, "A little hair of the dog that bit me."

"What?" whispered Polly.

"You know. They say you should drink a taste of whatever you drank the night before. It always makes a headache go away. I like vodka because it doesn't make your breath smell so obvious."

"Mo, are you drinking alone?" asked Polly.

Mo continued to pour.

From the kitchen, a key could be heard in the front lock. The front door swung open.

"Harvey!" chimed the bridge players.

Mo rushed from the kitchen and threw her arms around her husband. "Long time no see," she laughed.

The three guests excused themselves. "We'll just let you two get reacquainted," suggested Polly.

As the last of the bridge club closed the front door, Harvey kissed his wife. "You girls had quite a time I see."

Mo stiffened. "What do you expect? How long have you been away this time, three weeks, four?" She pulled herself away.

"I've missed you, too," he said, taken aback.

"Sure you did," she answered, downing her drink.

Harvey tried to put his arms around her.

"Get away from me," she said pushing him away with both hands. He tripped over a footstool and fell backwards onto the floor.

"Harvey! Are you all right?" asked Mo as she stooped down toward her husband. "It's, it's just that I didn't expect you home today. You didn't let me know."

Harvey sat on the floor saying nothing.

"Harvey?"

He looked up at Mo and said, "I wanted to surprise you, but I guess the surprise was on me."

During the next years, Harvey continued to travel. He was usually gone for weeks at a time. He missed birthdays, even their anniversary once. He called home, but often Mo wasn't there or didn't choose to answer the phone. Eventually Harvey brought home news that they needed to move.

"Honey, I can't help it," he pleaded with her. "We have to move, it's a big part of my job to be flexible," he explained.

"Well, I'm not so *flexible*! Damn your job, Harvey, and damn the company," shouted Mo. "I love New Orleans!"

"I know you do," said Harvey.

After much accusing, complaining and a good amount of angry silence, Mo acquiesced to Baton Rouge. She left behind her friends, Aunt Hattie, and Sarah. Mo amazed every one and adjusted rather well. Sometimes Harvey thought the change was good for her and perhaps, even good for their marriage. As Mo made a few friends, her trips back to New Orleans began to dwindle.

But then, one Friday night, Harvey came home with the news that he had been told he must agree to transfer again. This time they'd be farther away from New Orleans; they were going to Jackson, Mississippi.

"Good grief," Mo responded, "are there even paved roads there?"

Another few months and another move. "Mo, now don't get upset, but we've got to move to Birmingham."

She was too angry to hear any details. She stormed out to her car, got in, and drove away. "The son-of-a-bitch is moving me again," she screamed to herself.

Mo never mentioned a word about being unhappy to her mother. She simply drank and sought out new friends every place the Clarks were transferred. The number of moves grew to nearly one each year. After the next three or four new towns, Mo stopped trying. She made no efforts to make friends. She only made certain she knew the location of a grocery store, a liquor store, and the Catholic Church. She always found comfort in going to Mass.

As it turned out, Harvey wasn't at all like Eugene as Sarah had hoped he'd be. He was ambitious and successful, and seemingly deeply in love with Mo. But most assuredly, the husband did not consider his wife's needs. Oblivious to his beautiful young wife's escalating isolation, he only knew that when he came back from his long business trips, Mo was home to welcome him. Sometimes, she was sober. That was their routine until 1944 and WWII.

"Drafted! My God, Harvey, you're going to be thirty-four years old on your next birthday. Aren't you too old to be in the Army?" demanded Mo.

"Doesn't look that way," responded the shaken man. "I've got the papers to prove that right here."

For a few minutes neither could talk. Then, uncharacteristically, Harvey took his wife in his arms and held her for a very long time. Mo sobbed. Later they went quietly to bed.

After basic training, Harvey got his orders to go to Germany. At the train station the day he was to ship off, Mo pretended that her husband was merely going on another business trip.

The train's engine revved up as hundreds of young men embraced wives, kissed their children and said goodbye to families for the last time. "I'm sorry, Mo," Harvey said to Mo as her fingers pulled away from his grip. "I'm sorry."

As the train rumbled out of the station, Mo swallowed hard. Her emotions, she guessed, were making her ill. She swallowed again, but to no avail. Mo raced to the ladies room and vomited. Funny, she hadn't had a drink in days.

Mo returned to New Orleans and moved in with her mother. A month later, she went to the doctor. After ten years of marriage, she had some news.

"Mother, I'm pregnant," she announced. She quickly downed a Coke flavored with a shot of bourbon and burst into tears.

Sarah's mouth dropped open.

Mo was terrified. "Hell of a note, how am I going to get through this without Harvey?" she moaned.

At first, Sarah could say nothing. How could Imogene handle this? The fact was she couldn't. Not Imogene.

In a truck on a road somewhere on the outskirts of Frankfurt, Germany, Harvey read the news via a telegram from his wife: HARVEY—HURRY HOME—A BABY IS DUE IN FEBRUARY—LOVE— MOMMIE.

3

February 6, 1945, a six-pound baby girl was born to the Clarks. Without waiting to hear her husband's opinion, Mo named the child Sarah Imogene Sinclair Clark II.

Initially, the tiny black-haired, red-faced three-week premature infant was called "Little Mo." Within days, Sarah's pre-birth apprehension was completely forgotten by the delighted grandmother who fell head over heels in love with the baby.

Mo, however, was still not feeling "maternal." So, two weeks later, when mother and child were sent home from the hospital, Aunt Hattie, nearing age eighty, came over to help every day. A practical nurse was also hired as Sarah hurried through her workday to care for the infant at night. During those early morning hours of bottle-feeding and burping, Sarah forged a bond with the tiny girl that would last throughout her life.

The doting grandmother liked everything about her grandchild but the name "Little Mo." Sarah could stand it no longer, so one evening she casually suggested to Imogene that it might be less confusing for everybody if the baby were called by a different name. The new mother didn't feel like arguing. Sarah began to refer to the baby by her initials: S. I. S. Some days it would be "Sissie," others, "Little Sis." Finally, "Sister" was what best suited everyone, especially Sarah.

"You need a name, Mother," suggested Mo. "How about 'Grandmother'?"

"I'm not sure I am ready to give up my real name. What do you think about 'Grandmother Sarah'?"

"Sounds like a mouthful," said Mo, "but suit yourself."

One Sunday morning, as she rocked Sister, Sarah starting thinking about what her daughter had said. "'Grandmother Sarah' would be hard for my precious little one to say," she whispered to the baby. "And, oh my dear, for you to learn to spell such a long name, for goodness sakes, it would be entirely too difficult! What do you think, dearest?" asked Sarah as she held Sister patting her tiny back.

Sister cooed.

"That's right, darling child. Let's just see. 'Grandma Sarah?' No. 'Grand?' There's no personality to that. 'Grandee'?"

The baby wiggled in her arms.

"Yes, Grandee it is then!"

Her very being began to revolve around the little granddaughter. "Grandee" replaced "Sarah" everywhere but in her office. Professionally, she would always be Sarah Sinclair.

She hadn't been a *wife* for thirteen years.

She refused to term herself a *widow*.

Sarah also felt uncomfortable with being *mother*, she relinquished that title because of Imogene's failings which she saw as her own.

She delighted in discovering herself as Grandee.

Now, Mo did love her baby. Her feelings of delight and amazement were manifested in her blue eyes each time she looked at little Sister. However, Mo was also terribly nervous about caring for the infant. Were she holding her, and Sister fretted the least bit, the new mother absolutely panicked and summoned the help of Aunt Hattie, or the nurse or Grandee.

Like countless thousands of other women whose husbands had joined the fight in World War II, Mo needed her child's father at her side. His absence was the one thing she would never forget. Harvey Clark was not there for the first six months of their daughter's life. Mo could never find it in her heart to forgive Harvey or to forgive "that idiot Adolph Hitler and his ridiculous Third Reich."

Each week, an increasingly more melancholy Mo wrote pleading letters to PFC Harvey Clark, not from herself, but from his baby girl. From age six weeks to her father's return when she was six months old, Sister would write messages such as

Dear Daddy,

I want you to come home! I'm getting bigger and prettier every day. Mommy says she and I love you, but we are awfully mad at you because you aren't here in New Orleans. Here is another Kodak picture of us.

We miss you, especially me,

Love,

Sister

The war finally ended for PFC Clark on August 13, 1945. His cab pulled up in front of Grandee's apartment around two o'clock that afternoon. Mo had placed Sister in the baby buggy and was getting ready to take her for a walk around the block. She saw the cab and stopped mid-step. "Harvey?"

A much thinner Harvey threw open the car door and sprinted across the front lawn. "Harvey!" Mo smiled broadly as she collapsed in his arms. Their first kiss was the sweetest of their ten-year marriage.

Beaming, Mo turned toward the buggy and said, "Look, Harvey, look what we got!"

His head swiveling back and forth from his baby to his wife, Harvey wasn't able to take it all in. All the months as he drove the military supply truck around Germany, all those frightening, lonely months were at long last over. Like tens of thousands of GIs, Harvey had awakened from the nightmare of war. The letters and the pictures had called him home, away from death and fear, and the blood and filth of the front. As if still dreaming in his makeshift bed in the back of his truck, PFC Clark, discharged, couldn't absorb enough as he continued to admire his beautiful wife and their adorable baby girl.

"I just can't believe how cute she is!" he exclaimed.

"Of course!" replied the ecstatic mother, "Everyone says she looks like you!"

Later in the day, they left a note for Grandee and drove away. For the first time in memory, the Clarks bypassed every bar in the city. They went instead to Lake Pontchartrain and sat under a tree holding hands. "It's so good to be home," Harvey repeated again and again. Like Mo and Grandee, he had fallen immediately in love with Sister. The two of them watched the baby play in Mo's handbag as the sun set on the glistening waters of the lake. For a while, at least, it appeared Harvey and Mo were themselves finally falling in love.

Harvey's company promised him he could remain in New Orleans for the next four to five years. So thrilled were Mo and Harvey, they decided to purchase a home of their own. Even Grandee soon moved into the Clarks' new bungalow on Hector Avenue because she didn't want anything to separate her from Sister. Harvey took his mother-in-law's presence in stride.

As the memories of war faded into peace and summer faded into fall, Mo went into a frenzy getting ready for their first Christmas in the house and as a family of three, or four counting Grandee. The war was over and the future was a bright one for most Americans, most certainly, including the Clarks.

Mo prepared for a visit from Santa Claus by selecting a plush brown teddy bear with black button eyes. She tied a green satin bow around his chubby, fuzzy neck. "Won't little Sister just love him!" she said.

Harvey smiled approvingly as his exultant wife showed off her purchase. "The bear is as big as Sister," he laughed.

Mo spent days readying her holiday cards. Each time she signed one she felt contentment: *Love to you and yours, from Harvey, Mo, and our cutie pie, "Sister."*

Christmas Eve, as Grandee kept watch over Sister in her baby bed, Harvey went down to the basement and retrieved the shiny Radio Flyer wagon from its hiding place behind a stone wall. Mo hummed carols while she worked to fill Sister's new red stocking with a white stenciled Santa riding atop his reindeer-drawn sleigh. She and Harvey, both giggling, managed to eat most of the candy as they arranged the not yet one-year old's gifts under their tree.

Within a couple of years, however, Harvey's job began pulling him back into his old pre-war patterns, back into a routine of business trips that took him away for weeks on end. Mo's displeasure grew proportionally.

As Sister developed into a little girl, she and her father spent Sunday mornings at Audubon Park. While Mo attended Mass,

Harvey and his daughter had their own time together at the zoo.

"Oh, Daddy, isn't there some way to see the tigers without having to walk by those awful sea lions?" pleaded Sister. "They make so much noise."

"I'm afraid not, honey. Come on, now hold my hand. Be brave with me."

Sister took her father's hand. "I just get to have you sometimes, Daddy. I want you here, all the time," Sister pouted.

Harvey looked down at his daughter. "You're your Mommie's daughter," he insisted.

"Yours, too, Daddy," Sister countered as the pair skirted the sea lions' enclosure.

"Look, Sister," Harvey said quickly, "we've gotten past the sea lions, and they hardly barked at all."

"Maybe they are sleeping like Mommie does sometimes after she gets real loud."

Harvey stopped. Kneeling down beside his child, he said, "All mommies and daddies yell sometimes."

Sister hung her head.

Harvey put his hands under her chin and lifted her face. Looking into his daughter's eyes he said, "Your Mommie and Daddy are going to try to be more like those sea lions today and be quieter. Okay?"

"Okay, Daddy."

"Let's go see how Fatima's doing today?" Harvey suggested, pointing toward the elephants' pen.

An old bachelor friend of Harvey's came to town on business. Instead of going to the zoo, Harvey took Sister to see his friend in a bar down on Canal Street. "Baby, let's do something different today," her father urged. "The paper says that Fatima is on vacation this week."

"Is Tima at the beach, like us sometimes, Daddy?" asked Sister.

"Yes," replied her father. "Your elephant's out in the Gulf of Mexico," he laughed.

When Mo returned home from church, Sister greeted her mother and said, "Mommie, listen, listen to this." Before Harvey could stop her, she joyfully sang for her mother the new song that the waitress taught her when she took her to the ladies room. "Goodnight, Irene, Irene. Good night, Irene. Good night, Irene, Irene, I'll see you in my dreams." Sister beamed with pride.

"So, Fatima sings now?" said Mo glaring daggers at Harvey.

"Mo, it was harmless, we just stopped down at—," Harvey began.

"*Harmless*? You took our daughter to a *bar*?" Mo accused. "Harvey, that's not *harmless*."

"You're one to talk, Mo. Where were you Friday night when I got home?" Harvey demanded. "I smelled the glass. You were passed out asleep!"

"Stop! Daddy, you promised!" Sister cried as she ran from the kitchen.

Harvey went away for a long business trip that same afternoon, and later that week, Mo spent all day in bed.

Often, Sister would go out to the backyard making her way past the banana trees toward her father's gravel pile. She had burrowed her own little spot in the gravel that fit perfectly the outline of her body. She snuggled down in it and stretched her arms and legs to rest. Sister liked to lie in her rock cocoon and sing as the sun went down. It gave her a feeling of security, especially when Mo and Harvey would fight over Harvey's travel. Sister sang softly, "The sky is pink and blue, the sky is pink and blue, the sky is pink and blue, blue-ue-ue."

Mo was never much on discipline which gave Sister more freedom than other children with whom she played. Sister's playmate Francie was six years old. Francie's mother expected her to help with dusting and work in the kitchen. Jeannie's mom was even more demanding. Jeannie actually had to baby sit with her twin, wild-as-the-wind, three-year-old brothers.

It wasn't only that she was excused from helping out, occasionally Sister was actually encouraged to misbehave. There was an incident with the lady next door. Sister's friend Jeannie, the girl with the twin brothers, dared her to grab the neighbor's tacky, red velvet, fake emerald-decorated bedroom slippers and hide them. Sister got the ugly things and pitched them into the banana grove. Not experienced in criminal acts, the five-year old was caught immediately. She couldn't find the shoes, so Mo was called over.

"Sister, I am surprised at you!" said her mother. Mo acted furious. "We'll just go right downtown and buy our nice neighbor a replacement pair," she offered.

Head down, Sister nodded yes. Her lip quivered.

"All right then," snapped the neighbor.

"How 'bout this pair?" said Mo later at the shoe store.

"Mommie, I *am* sorry," offered Sister, "but those are so ugly."

"I know," giggled Mo. "We'll take them," she told the clerk.

The replacements were purple, covered in a rainbow of jewels with gold piping.

When they went back to deliver the slippers and apologize to the angry lady, Mo shook her head back and forth lamenting, "I just don't know what got into her. Sister, say you're sorry." Mo looked at her daughter and frowned.

Sister, teary-eyed, whispered, "Yes, ma'am. And I'll never be bad again."

When they went back inside, things changed. Mo gave her little girl a glass of lemonade, her own included a jigger of vodka. The two of them shared an early dinner of cheese toast and grapes. Mo enjoyed more adult lemonade. She motioned to Sister to sit by her at the window and said, "Let's have some fun, honey." Mo raised the window and called out to the neighbor. "Old Miss Prune Face better watch out. We're gonna get your purple slippers if you leave them outside again!" Sister had to hold her tummy she was laughing so hard.

Mo had a nightcap, and Sister finished the grapes.

Sometimes Sister believed that her mother was actually an angel, a grownup-sized playmate that she had been given for her very own. Sister saw herself as the charmed little princess, a princess just as Grandee described her mother to be when she was a little girl.

Should Sister try to set the table, Mo would say, "No, honey, you go on and play now. Mommie doesn't want you to ruin your pretty little hands." Not much was asked of her except, "Mommie is tired, go amuse yourself quietly." More and more frequently, Sister couldn't wake her mother when she "rested" on the living room sofa.

One winter morning Mo decided to cook a pot roast even though Harvey was away on business in Mississippi. Pleased with her idea, she treated herself to an early cocktail. She floured and peppered the beef and put it in a cast iron skillet atop the gas stove. Mo saluted her accomplishment by pouring a second cocktail.

Grandee had called earlier hoping to stay downtown to attend a play. Would Imogene mind? "Of course not," she answered. "Sister and I will get along just fine." The roast sizzled in its juices. It smelled wonderful; she finished that drink and poured another. Mo turned the flame to simmer and sat for awhile to read a magazine.

Hours passed, it was starting to get dark outside. Sister had played quietly all day, just as she had been told to do, but her stomach was beginning to growl. She hadn't had lunch. Mo had retreated to her room after a few more drinks. Her door was closed. Sister could almost taste the meat sizzling in the kitchen. Her stomach grumbled again.

Sister went in the kitchen and reached for the peanut butter. She decided instead to see what was cooking in the big black skillet. With both hands she grasped the handle. Hot as fire, it seared the tender skin of her fingers and palms. Tears streamed down her cheeks. Sister released her unbearable grip; the whole thing—skillet, roast, juices, the top—crashed down onto the floor. "Mommie!" shrieked the injured child.

No response came from behind the closed bedroom door. Only the hum of the floor fan was audible. Sister stood in the center of the kitchen in the hot puddle of juices and grease. She inspected her tiny, red, raw hands and shook them wildly to throw off the terrible pain. Her pulse racing, her body began to tremble. The little girl dropped to the floor and wept.

Minutes passed. Still no response came from Mo. Sister curled up into a ball. A half-hour went by, but there was no sign of her mother. Sister's stomach growled again and again. Her head throbbed as hunger eventually won over the pain of her burning hands. Sister climbed, her knees on a stool, and retrieved a cold, wet, soapy rag from her mother's dishpan. The cool water felt good to her hands.

She wrapped her right hand in the dripping cloth and crossed the kitchen to the drawer where she had watched her mother get the silver. Water from the rag dripped into the splattered gravy. Using the unburned tips of her thumb and finger, she seized the end of a salad fork. Sister squatted on the floor next to the skillet and tried to hold the fork. She couldn't.

"*Darn!*" cried Sister. Frustrated and famished, Sister flung the fork.

Lowering her face to the ruined dinner, the child gnawed the roast. Holding her hands well away up next to her shoulders, she tore at the meat with her teeth. Her nose, her cheeks, her chin, and lips were covered in juice and pieces of beef. Sister's hair dropped over into the skillet but that didn't slow her. She simply raised her head a second to shake her hair out of her mouth.

When Grandee got home from the play, she found the filthy, injured child asleep on the cold floor by the skillet. "My God," she gasped. She gently woke her and walked her into the bathroom. She closed the lid of the toilet and, having Sister sit on it, whispered, "Precious darling, let Grandee help you."

At first, the child drew back her hands. "I'm sorry, Grandee, I didn't mean to make a mess," she pleaded.

Grandee choked back her shock when she unwrapped Sister's hands. She carefully bathed the little girl and soaked her burned hands with cold water. "Oh, Sister," said Grandee as she fought back her own tears, "you did nothing wrong! This will make everything feel better. Tell Grandee if this hurts my baby."

Sister's eyes riveted on her hands. She said nothing.

Her grandmother patted dry the child's tiny hands and coated them with ointment. She tenderly rocked her just as she had when Sister was small. When her granddaughter drifted off to sleep, she carried her to bed. Grandee sat by her side all through the night.

In the morning, she slid a note under Imogene's door. There was no admission of guilt from Mo either to the child or to Grandee, but she again became the ideal playmate the little girl believed to be an angel. Because Sister's hands had to be bandaged for a few days, Mo watched over her like a mother bird. Together they colored and played games. They drank Cokes, without the flavor of bourbon added to Mo's. And on the day the doctor said Sister was able to go without her bandages, they celebrated by going downtown to buy new dresses for Sister's two best baby dolls.

4

Harvey was in Mississippi for three more weeks. It was decided that he shouldn't be told about what had happened. "Your Daddy would be so upset with us. Let's not worry him," cautioned Grandee. "It can be our secret."

Sister's hands didn't hurt anymore, and the blisters and red places were all healed. "All right," she agreed as she went back to playing with her doll.

When Harvey came home, he was driving a brand new company car. The whole family was excited and everyone went for a ride around the neighborhood. Mo sat in the front seat, Grandee and Sister in the back.

The next morning, just Harvey, Mo, and Sister went out together. Sister sat in the middle of the front seat between her parents. She examined her injured hands and could hardly tell where the burns had been. She turned her head and looked at her Daddy, then at her Mommie. The car windows were rolled down, the wind blew Mo's hair back. Harvey was telling her about his customer in Tupelo.

"Daddy, do your customers get to ride in your car like us?" she asked.

"Sure, but it's more fun when you are with me," he said, smiling at her.

"And Mommie and Grandee?"

"Oh yes, and Mommie and Grandee, too." He winked at Mo.

"So how come you have to spend so much time with customers, when you want to be with us?" argued Sister.

"Daddies don't always have a choice, baby." He pulled into the drugstore. "Say, how about some candy?" he asked.

He came out with a sack full of chocolates. On the way home Sister licked melted M&Ms off her fingers. As she licked, she could see her hands were healed.

A week or so later, Sister was again pleading with her father not to leave her. He had run out of explanations for his daughter. "Sweetheart, it's just Daddy's job, but I'll only be gone a week this time," Harvey said as he swallowed hard.

Sister cried as he backed down the driveway the next morning. She waved wildly as he drove away. She shouted, "See you Friday, Daddy? Promise? Promise!" He disappeared around the corner and his little girl counted off the days until her Daddy came back to her.

In the fall of 1951, Harvey's company transferred him to Memphis. The family made preparations to move—again. A sign was put in the yard as soon as the house was ready to be shown. It sold quickly.

Once in Memphis, the Clarks bought a house near family and friends who had been close to the Sinclair family for years. Sister was able to walk to the homes of her cousins and play with neighborhood children whose mothers had played with Mo when she was little.

Returning home made Mo Clark more miserable than she'd been since Harvey went overseas. Living in Memphis rekindled memories of a time when Imogene was her father's beloved princess. Being back served as a daily reminder that her days of being her own parents' single-treasured pearl were gone for good.

"How bout we go get a big triple scoop of butter pecan ice cream?" slurred Mo.

"I'm ready, Mommie, let's hurry," urged Sister. By age six, she was keenly aware that they should leave for the ice cream shop before her mother had a chance to sit down and doze off. She took her mother by the hand and led her out to the car.

Mo and Sister jumped into the family's green Pontiac and sped off in pursuit of the ice cream. Sister loved those trips. Mo drove fast. The little girl rolled the window as far down as it would go and hung out as far as she could, her knees anchored under the door's armrest. As they rounded the corner, the wind whirled her ponytails in circles.

At the ice cream shop, they ran into Mo's friend, Louise. She had ordered herself a double chocolate fudge sundae. Louise was savoring each bite that she followed with a puff from her Lucky Strike.

"Hallo, girls!" she yelled.

"Hello, Aunt Louise," whispered Sister.

"How ya be, Louise?" asked Mo as she checked the sign over the counter for the featured flavor of the week. "I'll have two scoops of butter pecan, if you please," she said. "And my little girl will have two scoops of chocolate."

Sister enjoyed being out and about as much as she liked eating ice cream. She loved to watch all the people, though it was curious to her that other ladies she saw in places like Howard Johnson didn't seem to be quite as noisy as her mother.

Mo and Louise were lost in their grownup conversation. Sister twirled her spoon carving tiny highways in her ice cream.

Mo finished and lit her cigarette. She blew a ring of smoke. Holding the cigarette loosely, Mo waved it about as she talked. She turned suddenly to check out someone coming into the shop, a friend, she thought at first. With her awkward gesture, the cigarette shot into Sister's left eye.

"For God's sake," Mo shrieked.

Sister assumed she had upset her mother. "I'm sorry," she cried, clutching both hands to her burnt eyelid.

Mo grabbed an ice cube from her water glass and began to cram it into the little girl's eye. Sister jerked her head back and forth. "It hurts, Mommie," she complained.

"Be still," ordered Mo.

Louise and Mo were only their noses' length from Sister when she opened both eyes to try to focus. "See, Mo," assured Louise. "She's perfectly fine, just a little burn on the lid. It may not leave a scar."

"I need a drink," said Mo.

Sister's ice cream was left to melt.

Things that injured her child seemed to get Mo's attention. So again, as she had in New Orleans, the mother attempted to pull herself together without the aid of alcohol. This time she found a new focus, her yard.

The Clark's home was built at the end of a circle, so their backyard fanned out on either side. The property was nearly an acre in size, and Mo was determined to fill the area with flowers, trees and shrubbery. Gardening became her obsession.

On the right side of the fan, she had Harvey construct an English rose garden. Brick paths angled around toward a concrete bench in the center which was decorated with multi-colored pieces of cracked tile. Fragrant roses in varying shades of red surrounded the outer borders while smaller ones of peach and yellow were placed toward the middle. Tiny pink tea roses circled the bench leaving just enough room for someone to sit without being scratched by thorns.

Covering the left side of the fence and across the back, Mo put in row after row of irises. The new gardener poured through her stacks of flower catalogues, ordering anything that appealed to her. Mo came alive with her flowers as they began to bloom. Like a Monet painting, her yard became a vista of colors ranging from snow white, yellow, pink, and red, to violet, brilliant blue, and dark purple. Basket in hand, Mo went out early every morning to gather fresh flowers. She pinched off the dead blooms explaining, "Removing the faded ones will encourage new growth."

In the center of the backyard and away from the flower beds, Sister's swing set was erected. She played on the trapeze and rode her sky scooter as she watched her mother tend to her garden. Sometimes, Mo went inside and got a beer for herself and a Coke for Sister. The two would relax in the shade.

Harvey made it his habit to tour the yard with his wife as soon as he arrived back in town from a business trip. They would stroll together as Mo proudly showed off her "toonies." On Saturdays and Sundays, Harvey did his part to keep up the expansive yard. He cut the lawn, planted dogwood trees, and built a barbeque pit out of concrete blocks. As neither Harvey nor Mo liked to cook, the pit proved to be a greater success as Sister's "wilderness fort" than it was a place to barbeque.

Mo's old school chums had grown into the wives and mothers of Memphis society. The St. Agnes Academy *girls* who once ran with Mo now used their free time to fill volunteer positions throughout the community. They assumed, of course, that Mo would join them. Her fellow alums from St.

Agnes encouraged her to sign up to donate her time to the school.

"Gracious, Mo, you and Sarah are graduates, and now Sister is third generation. You really must," they urged. Her old friends also saw to it that Mo was invited to join the Madonna Circle, an enthusiastic group which supported the children of Saint Peter's Orphanage.

Neither St. Agnes nor the Madonna Circle were Mo's cup of tea. She frequently forgot to show up at the meetings. When she was asked to spend time working at a bake sale or to drive one of the orphans to a dental appointment, she generally offered instead to donate a piece of the Sinclair family crystal.

The yard was lovely.

Very little of the crystal remained.

At the grocery store one Monday, Sister noticed a case of beer in her mother's cart under the paper towels and cereal. Excited at the prospect of company coming, she asked, "Mommie, are we having a party?"

"Uh-huh," Mo responded.

No guests came to share the beer.

Harvey advanced to the position of regional sales manager of his company. He traveled all around the Southeast, leaving each Sunday and returning on Friday. No matter how late it was when her father got home for the weekends, Sister was allowed to stay up with him for the "Friday Night Fights." Mo usually went to bed.

The black-and-white RCA television in the center of the living room was the focal point of their father-daughter Fridays. When the boxing matches were over, and if Harvey and Sister weren't too sleepy, they stayed up to watch *My Little*

Margie. Sister hardly ever admitted she was sleepy. She liked to imagine she was Margie, pretending to be the beautiful grownup daughter who lived in the big city apartment house with her handsome, white-haired father. On the show, and in her imagination, the daddy was always at home, and no one ever slurred her speech.

Grandee wrote to her Imogene that Mr. Jones was going to retire from his law practice, so her secretarial job would soon end. She was considering a move to Memphis. Once Sister heard about that possibility, there was no choice to be made. "Grandee, are you coming next week?"

The Clarks offered to add an apartment onto their home for her. Grandee liked the idea. Sister began to count off the days until her grandmother would be living one flight of stairs away.

When the construction was finished and Mr. Jones officially retired, Harvey arranged to go to New Orleans on business so he could drive his mother-in-law to Memphis. On a Sunday afternoon, he brought Grandee home. Sister bolted out the front door to greet them. She usually jumped into her father's arms, but that day she went right for her grandmother. "Grandee! Grandee!"

"Hello, my little darling," said Grandee climbing from the car as quickly as she could. "My, but look how big you've grown!"

"Hurry, Grandee, I have so much to show you."

"Let's get started then," she replied. "I've got all the time you want."

"Wanna swing?"

"On your new swing set? Of course, I do," she said.

Mo walked across the lawn to greet her mother. "Sister, please, honey, your grandmother has been in the car all day long. Let her catch her breath."

"Paa-shaw," said Grandee. "Let's go swing!" Grandee and Sister made their way to Sister's swing set among Mo's flowers. "My goodness, won't you look at your Mommie's garden!" said Grandee.

Mo smiled.

"When you get through swinging with our girl, Sarah, do come and see what you think about your new home," invited Harvey.

After a few weeks, Sarah Sinclair found a job at the Ellis Auditorium as executive secretary to the manager. Sister reluctantly approved of her going back to work. "Good for you," she said, trying to be cheerful. She had enjoyed having her around all the time. "I guess you're in charge of Memphis like Daddy's in charge of Tennessee. I'm glad you'll come home at night."

Five and a half days a week, Sarah Sinclair caught the city bus to her job at the auditorium. After work, she arrived at her stop and walked the two blocks down Montclair Drive to the Clark's house on the circle. Most days, Sister met her half way. Her grandmother often had news that the ice show was in town or that an opera or even the circus would be coming to the auditorium.

Sister knew her grandmother was very important because the two of them not only got to go to the circus, the ice show and to other exciting events, but they were also given the best seats in the house. Of course, there was the down side to Grandee's status. They got the choice seats, but Sister had to be the victim of the show's pranks.

"Oh no, oh no," fretted Sister. "Here he comes, that creepy scary clown."

Grandee smiled slyly in her seat. "Here, darling, let me hold your cotton candy for you."

The spotlight blinded everyone in the front row where they sat and for several rows behind them. The announcer blared in his universal voice, "No, Bruno, don't do it. You'll get water all over that little girl! Look out, ladies and gentlemen. Look out, little girl!"

Confetti covered Sister. She flushed red as she attempted to brush the shredded paper out of her hair and off her dress. Everyone in the arena erupted with laughter.

The spotlight flashed back to the ice skaters. The voice continued, "It's okay, folks, it wasn't water after all!"

"Grandee, I think the clown was after *you* this time," Sister suggested.

Sometimes on school mornings, Mo overslept which meant Sister would be late for school *again*. *Some*times grew into *often*times. Every now and again, Mo slept in strange places, places like in the middle of the backyard or on the living room floor.

Sister loved school and the nuns because she knew they never drank beer or vodka. They were much too busy loving the little girls they taught, too busy playing pianos as the girls sang, too busy listening, too busy praising essays or artwork for a bulletin board, too busy cheering for the "pigtail" basketball team, and too busy urging a newly chosen actress to speak out more clearly, to "e-nun-ci-ate."

The second graders told the first graders that the Dominicans had no legs. So intrigued was Sister by the mysterious holy women, she almost believed the rumor was true. She watched closely as the nuns floated about the classroom in their long white habits. Not one made a sound when walking, only the clacking of black wooden rosary beads signaled each teacher's whereabouts.

Sister wondered if the nuns could be angels.

Sister Agnes Ricarda had taken the first and second graders to her music room. As the children practiced their carols for the Christmas musical, Sister Clark kept her eyes riveted on the smiling nun. She tapped her baton on the pedestal, "Young ladies, are we all ready?"

"Yes, Sister Agnes Ricarda," they chanted.

She raised the baton.

"O come, all ye faithful," sang the little slightly-off-key voices in unison. The nun glowed in the glory of her singing cherubs. Her arms flew up as her baton touched the ceiling of the room and Sister spotted the shoes underneath the nun's habit. Without thinking, Sister exclaimed, "Feet! Sister Agnes Ricarda, you do have feet!"

The second grade girls giggled. The first graders made faces at the older students. "You told us a story!" they accused.

The second graders giggled all the more.

"Young ladies!" clapped the nun. "Order! We must have order!"

The room quieted. All eyes shifted to Sister. She wanted to melt into the linoleum floor.

"Well, Sarah Imogene, what is this about my feet?" she said showing the little girl the full extent of one of her long black oxfords.

Sister gasped as did the children around her.

"I—I thought angels could fly," she stammered.

Sister Agnes Ricarda burst into laughter. "Oh, I see! The big girls got you children with that silly story again this year!" She hugged Sister. "As you can see, I am most definitely earthbound, at this point anyway, darling girl. Perhaps some day we will *all* be in heaven, dear child. But today we must ready ourselves for our Christmas concert." She returned to her podium, chuckled again, and raised her baton.

After that day, Sister was even more certain the nuns were angels. She supposed they took off those big shoes when planning to fly.

At St. Agnes, the children were encouraged to "dedicate" their papers by writing spiritual messages on the top of the first page. Most students chose to write the letters "JMJ," dedicating the work to Jesus, Mary, and Joseph. Sister's dedication was different. She wrote "PSM" at the top of her papers. Each year, her new teacher would ask the question, "Sarah Imogene, now share with us. What does 'PSM' mean, dear?"

Sister never let it be known, because it was her secret. As safe as she felt at school, she could not reveal what, most likely, the intuitive nuns had figured out. She would not tell them that all her school work was offered to PSM...Please Stop Momma.

At home, she was often hungry. At home, she was worried that someone might come by, an adult to see Momma or a friend to play with Sister. How many times did Sister help her mother into the back of the house to hide her from the person on the other side of the ringing doorbell? How many times did she lie to the caller, "Momma is busy and can't come to the phone. May I take a message?"

Most of her hours at home were spent finding ways to escape, often to the Harrison's house with its four little girls, a daddy, and a mother who made peanut butter and jelly sandwiches. Or she went over to Pat's. Her mom liked to sing along with popular music on the radio. Or she played with friends from school, always at *their* homes. She played with JoAnn or Betty, or with one of the others—all who had homes with mothers who wouldn't be staggering around and cursing or passed out cold.

On days Sister had to play at home due to fever, chicken pox, or a similar malady, she would erect a card table tent. She'd use two of her Grandmother Clark's handmade quilts for the roof and sides. Once secure in the cloth walls of her home within the house, Sister read for hours by flashlight.

Her favorite escape was climbing the pull-down stairs and disappearing into her own world of toys, dolls, and doll furniture in her attic playroom. She got to where she could hoist the stairs halfway back up for complete privacy.

It was in the attic where Sister set up her elaborate Roy Rogers ranch set with its plastic horses, fences, cowboys, and, best of all, the two cowgirls, Dale Evans and Annie Oakley. Her layout spanned the length of the floored part of the attic and included mountains made of cardboard, mirror lakes, dirt planting fields enclosed in shirt box tops, a ranch house and a metal barn with a corral where the horses were penned. Directly in the center of the corral, Sister placed one of the cowgirls astride her fine Palomino as he galloped among the less notable steeds.

The one toy she kept downstairs was her dollhouse. Originally, it was beige particleboard trimmed with brown paint to look like English Tudor. Red roses were stenciled on haphazardly in the manufacturer's attempt to decorate it. "Daddy," Sister pleaded, "Could you do something to fix up my dollhouse? I want it to look more cheerful."

Harvey Clark lovingly renovated it to his daughter's specifications. He knocked out walls to create a great room, built a breakfast bar, and laid a linoleum floor. He painted the outside white and added green shutters to the five front windows and around the entry. He cut holes in each end to create windows for more light in the bedrooms that he painted—one yellow, one blue.

Sister was thrilled. She had watched his every step, and once the renovation was completed, she joyfully moved in her little plastic family. "There, don't you just love your new home?" she said as she placed each piece of plastic furniture. "Oh, Daddy, I'm so happy. Thank you," she said as she put the dollhouse daddy in his easy chair by the fireplace. She placed the girl on the sofa close to him.

For eight years, first through eighth grade, while the Clarks lived in Memphis, Sister and Margaret Harrison, the second of the Harrison girls, played every day. The girls' mother, Mary Catherine had been friends with Mo since their own days at St. Agnes. Like their mothers before them, Sister and Margaret spent hours exploring their shared neighborhood and, without anyone's permission, wandered for miles around, on foot, on bicycle, on skates. An average day would begin with a phone call.

"Can you come over?" said Margaret.

"I'm on my way," squealed Sister.

"Bring your bike," ordered Margaret. "Bye."

"Okay. Bye." With that, Sister was out the door. The girls rode their bikes up High Point Terrace, up Walnut Grove, and all the way to Highland across to the biggest shopping center in east Memphis. As they pedaled in front of the Plaza Theater, Sister announced, "I'm having a picture show party for my birthday next year. Can you come?"

Margaret blew a huge pink bubble. It popped covering her nose and down all over her chin. "Sure."

On they went.

In Sister's yard, they built forts and playhouses. By the railroad tracks that ran behind Sister's house, the two of them once dug a hole so deep and wide they both could squeeze inside. Margaret put her ear to the tracks. "I hear it!" she said. "Quick, into the hole."

They crouched way down and hid as the afternoon train approached.

As it crossed High Point Terrace, it blew the whistle, "Whoooooo, Woo!"

The girls shook with excitement.

In summer, Margaret, Sister, and their playmates lived outside. The girls used enough water jumping through sprinklers and squirting one another that the level of the nearby Mississippi River probably dropped. They wrote and starred in one-act plays, acted out movies they had seen, and also started and ended and started again club after club.

The biggest event the girls ever planned was a talent show to which five streets of neighbors were invited. The girls decided to publicize the show with their own handmade posters that they nailed on a number of trees and telephone poles throughout the area.

> Friday night, 7 o'clock at the Harrisons' house!
> Come and see the greatest talent in Memphis.
> You'll enjoy music, dance, funny stuff.
> Be there early to get a good seat.
> **Admission 25 cents**

Sister peeked out from behind the curtain. She spotted her father in the Harrisons' kitchen. He was shaking the popcorn pot on the eye of her electric stove. Sister looked around the room. The audience chatted with one another as they sat in metal folding chairs awaiting the beginning of the show. She counted forty-eight people. There would be forty-nine once her mother arrived. Grandee had saved a place for Mo.

"We're just about ready to start!" bubbled Margaret nervously.

"My mother's not here yet!" said Sister. "Let's wait just a minute. Please!"

"Well, okay, I guess," said Margaret.

Sister darted out from behind the curtain and squatted down at Grandee's feet. "Where's Momma?"

"I don't know, little darling," said Grandee, "but I'm here."

Sister ran into the kitchen and tugged on Harvey's shirt. "Daddy, where's Momma?"

Harvey sighed and replied, "Your mother wasn't feeling good." He shook the popcorn. *Pop! pop, pop, pop!* White kernels overflowed onto the stovetop. He grabbed the brown paper sacks, and he and Mrs. Harrison quickly began to fill them. She whispered in Sister's ear, "Mr. Harrison and I will be watching you, too."

Sister ran back to the stage. "Okay, Margaret, let's get going."

Mary Catherine, Margaret's older sister, went out front and the audience clapped. "Ladies and gentlemen, we want to welcome you to the greatest talent show you'll ever see! First, we have my very own little sister, Elizabeth Harrison, who will perform *Swan Lake.*" The audience was duly impressed. The next two acts were not nearly as well practiced, but each was received with equal enthusiasm. The first was a juggler with two balls, one of which was dropped and rolled under the sofa. The second was a ventriloquist whose lips moved, especially when she started to laugh.

Mary Catherine came out to introduce Tom's brother, Donnie, who was three years old. Suddenly, she heard a "Psst, psst."

"Excuse me, please!" she said. She ran back into the utility room that was doubling as a dressing room. "He what?" she asked.

Donnie was supposed to recite a poem about a sailboat, but he couldn't go on. He drank too much cherry Kool-Aid and wet his pants.

"Ladies and gentlemen, there has been a change in the show. We will now see Pat twirling her baton."

The girls delighted in their tapping, singing, and other acts. Sister did a pantomime to a Judy Garland song. At its end, the audience applauded warmly. After the applause for Sister died down, a slurred "Bravo" echoed from the back of the Harrison's family room.

"Mo, sit down, please!" said Harvey.

"Did you see her?" shouted Mo. "I thought she was terrrrific!" said Mo ignoring her husband's pleas. "Bravo, bravo, Sister Clark!"

Sister bowed. Her face turned crimson. Grandee slid down in her seat and pretended to be looking for something in her purse.

Donnie threw up in a Santa hat.

5

Even if she were busy playing, Sister checked her wristwatch as it grew closer to the time for the High Point Terrace bus to drop off Grandee. Sister usually stopped whatever she was doing and ran to meet her grandmother. Together they walked home.

If the Harrisons were playing outside on their hill, Sister would wave as she and Grandee passed saying, "See you later."

"Call after supper," said Margaret.

"Okay," Sister answered with no idea whether she would feel like calling her best friend later or not. She never knew how things would be at her house. Sister tramped down Montclair with her grandmother, but neither she nor Grandee ever expressed their worries out loud. They'd tell one another about their days as they walked along not once mentioning Mo.

Sister slowly pushed open the front door.

"Momma?" she whispered.

No answer.

"Imogene?' said Grandee a bit louder. No sound. Grandee's shoulders relaxed and she let her breath out slowly.

Frequently, Grandee made peanut butter and tomato sandwiches for the two of them. Peanut butter, tomato, and mayonnaise. Sometimes, it was roast beef with mayonnaise on saltine crackers.

Later, the pair would work on Sister's homework. Even when school wasn't in session, Grandee worked with her granddaughter on spelling or had her practice "real writing" until Sister formed the letters to perfection. Sister fussed sometimes, but she appreciated her grandmother's attention. Sometimes, Sister read as Grandee sat at her sewing machine making clothes for her growing army of dolls. At "break time," she'd direct her granddaughter to the dresser drawer where she kept candy, gum, pencils, and a variety of surprises. When Sister was upset about anything, likely whatever had happened upstairs, she found refuge at Grandee's.

The little girls of St. Agnes Academy all gathered around the two nuns who were in charge of the annual May Procession. Dressed in their Easter outfits, the girls prepared to march two by two across the St. Agnes campus as they sung hymns in honor of the mother of Jesus.

The girls all wore flowers in their hair. Some had silk roses, while others wore a band of real flowers, and some sported plastic daisies from Woolworth's. Sister was mortified. Hers was an enormous crown of roses intertwined with ivy and honeysuckle vines. She'd grown two inches that year. With the added flowers piled atop her head, she thought she looked like a trellis.

A few hours prior, Sister had overheard a conversation between Mo and Harvey.

"It is *Mother's* Day," Mo had complained. "I just didn't want to have to get up and go to that school today."

"Shhhh," said Harvey as he tried to quiet her. "Your daughter will hear you."

Sister didn't feel much like marching around to honor anyone's mother, not the mother of God, not her own.

"Come now, girls," said the nun. "It's time for us to begin."

The first and second grade girls came from behind the back of the school; next came the third and fourth graders; then Sister's class. Beaming parents lined the circular drive. Mothers, fathers, and grandparents "oohed and ahhed" as they proudly snapped pictures of their daughters and granddaughters.

"On this day, oh beautiful mother, on this day, we give you our love," Sister mouthed silently.

Someone's little brother pointed and shouted, "Look at that girl!" Sister just knew he was making fun of her. She stuck out her tongue.

The girls sang, "Ave, ave, ave Maria, Ave, ave Marrrriiiaa."

Sister spotted her family standing up on the left-hand side. She lowered her head and concentrated on her song sheet. As she peaked from behind the page, her eye caught Grandee's. Grandee grinned at her.

Sister smiled and slowly began to join in the singing.

"Grandee!" screamed Sister as she burst through the door at the top of the steps. She charged down. "Help, Grandee, Momma dumped out my dollhouse in the garbage!" yelled the little girl as she raced into the apartment.

"What?" replied the grandmother.

"Momma said they're coming tomorrow!" Sister shrieked.

"Who's coming, dear? Company?" queried Grandee.

"No, the garbage men. They're coming to get all my people! My dollhouse family and all their things, Grandee!" cried Sister.

Grandee shook her head back and forth as she looked at the little girl.

"I didn't mean to leave a mess. I didn't know Lizzie was coming to clean tomorrow. I'm sorry, truly I am!"

"Of course, you are," answered her grandmother. "We can take care of this."

"Why was Momma so mean?" pleaded Sister.

"I don't know, I just don't know."

Germs, thought Grandee as she patted her own chest in an effort to calm the both of them. She envisioned the garbage can, the big smelly gray metal garbage can, out by the carport. The can that reeked of spoiled meats and ruined green beans. The can that held days of coffee grounds and broken bottles. She pictured that can and inside she could imagine Sister's brown plastic daddy, the blue brother, the pale yellow sister and the dark pink mother, along with all the tiny pieces of furniture and accessories that Sister kept so lovingly arranged throughout the little house.

"Everything will be all right, little darling," Grandee told her grandchild. She grabbed a paper grocery bag and headed for the cans behind the fence gate, Sister in tow. Grandee said not another word but, holding a flashlight, dove headlong into the nasty metal can. Sister watched. In and out Grandee went, time after time until she managed to find the four people and each piece of their furniture, every lamp, and even the tiny dishes and cups.

Back inside, she washed each item in steaming hot soapy water in her kitchen sink. After she was sure everything was perfectly clean, she called to her granddaughter who was curled up on the daybed. "Come here, my darling, the two of us will dry your things, and you can put every single piece back just like you had it."

"Okay," sniffed the red-faced, tear-swollen child as she got up and crossed the linoleum tile floor.

"Now, where is the house, Sister?" the grandmother questioned cautiously as she handed her an extra towel.

"Momma dumped out my house in the garbage can," sniffed Sister. "I followed behind, all the time screaming for her to stop. Grandee, she wouldn't listen." Sister blew her nose. "She just kept saying bad words and fussing at me for my mess, and then she put the house down in the corner of my room real hard like she wanted to break it. I heard her bedroom door slam with a crash. That was when I came to get you."

As they dried together, Grandee added, "I believe the contents of your house needed a good spring cleaning anyway."

"Uh-huh," Sister sighed.

"See, everything looks better than before," Grandee pointed out. "Poor Imogene, she must not be feeling well tonight."

Sister didn't comment.

Before she went to bed, she wrote a "night-night" note to her father. He wasn't due back for three days, but she wrote anyway. As she perfectly formed every single letter of "Dear Daddy," she prayed her efforts would speed his return.

Dear Daddy,
I had a good day in school. I hope you had good customers on your business trip. I made the B-team in basketball. I'm a guard. Since I'm so tall, I can keep other girls from shooting. I guard better than I shoot.

Also, I stayed up during our Spelling Bee today. Three girls are left for tomorrow. Good luck to me!
I love you,
Your daughter, Sister

She didn't tell him about the dollhouse. Sister had learned to keep secrets.

Mo rarely mentioned her father. She was like her mother in that way, except Sarah never spoke Eugene's name. Usually, whatever Mo was willing to say she said during a long drive out to Calvary Cemetery. She took Sister there on special occasions like his birthday or at Christmas time. They always carried flowers to put on his grave—from her garden if it were warm, or a poinsettia, if it was cold outside. Afterwards, Mo, once thoroughly numbed with vodka, would go into her bedroom closet and retrieve the old Whitman's Sampler candy box. She would sit on the bed and slowly thumb through the contents that had long since replaced the original chocolates.

First, Mo gently removed a dried corsage, then, in order, came the weathered leather wallet that he carried, a half-empty package of cigarettes, and the picture enshrined in a gold broach. The picture was of her father, his arm around his dear little princess. She was smiling. In the photo, Imogene wore a graduation cap and gown. It was only one of two pictures that still existed of Eugene Sinclair. Both pictures of him were mostly blurs as if the man had faded into a mist.

Her fifth, sixth, and seventh grade years flew by as Sister busied herself with everything except what she had to face at home. She worked to make the best grades she could, played basketball, performed in school plays, and took dancing lessons. Sister began exchanging her time in the attic playroom for talking on the telephone. Boys became of increasing interest.

One afternoon, the Clark's phone rang.

"Hello," Sister answered.

Silence.

"Hello?" she repeated.

"Uhhhhh, this is Bill," stuttered the voice.

Sister's heart jumped from her chest. It was Bill from St. Dominic's, the Catholic boys school connected with St. Agnes. It was Bill from the ballroom dancing class. The tall, handsome Bill with blue-eyes. The "taller than she was" Bill.

"This is Sister," she gasped.

Silence.

More silence.

"Can you go with me to my Halloween dance?" he spit out.

"Yes!" squealed Sister.

Bill's mother drove the couple to the dance. They sat in the back seat, and when Bill held her hand, Sister could hardly catch her breath.

"You look pretty," Bill said.

"Thanks, this is new," she answered.

"Mom made me wear this dumb tie," he said.

Later, while they were dancing, Bill whispered in her ear, "My mother is PG."

"What's that?" asked Sister.

Bill blushed. Looking up at the gym ceiling, he said, "She's pregnant."

Sister swooned. That was the first thing she had ever heard a boy say that pertained to sex. She felt her face color. Sister couldn't talk for minutes. The next dance was a fast one. She loved it when the tall, blond boy swung her in a circle. Her skirt stood out all the way.

As she lay in bed that night, far too excited to sleep, Sister relived the whole evening. She remembered how easy it was to dance with a boy and that they could even talk at the same time. Sister wondered about Bill's mother. She'd seemed so sweet. *Pregnant.* None of her girlfriend's mother's were *that way.* It was as if all the children she knew were just, well, were just always there. She tried to think of Momma as *that way.* Momma? Pregnant? She couldn't imagine herself being inside of her mother's stomach.

That night she dreamed she was trapped inside a dark cavern. She couldn't move. The walls held her tightly. Monsters outside the cave were yelling. What they were saying, Sister couldn't quite hear.

6

"Got some good news, baby," announced Harvey as he came in from a business trip at the end of May.

"What, Daddy?" asked Sister.

"We're moving to Atlanta, Georgia." he beamed. "I got a big promotion."

Sister sank. "How far is that from Memphis?"

Her father asked, "What difference does that make?"

Sister knew there would be no reason to object. Daddy's job always came first. She didn't even try to argue.

Despite losing her darling Sister, Grandee chose to remain behind in Memphis, permanently. Instead, her grandmother found a nice apartment much closer to downtown Memphis. "See, little dear, your Grandee will have a shorter bus ride to the auditorium. And I'll only have to walk a quick few steps to my new place," she explained as she showed Sister around her new apartment.

Sister tried to be positive, "I like your front porch, Grandee."

"There you go, I can almost see a smile," she replied.

"No you can't," said Sister.

"Now Sister, do you see, my new house number on Monroe is 2186. Don't you remember, your new address in Atlanta will be 2086. They're almost the same."

When it came time for them to say good-bye, the grandmother and her grandchild struggled in their own way. "Oh, Grandee, I'll miss you so much," cried Sister. "What will

I do without you? I'll never pass a single test in that new high school without your help."

"Don't be so silly. You're nearly a grown up girl, fourteen years old, and plenty smart enough. You'll do just fine," she said stoically. "Sister, hush up now."

Grandee didn't allow herself to cry. She hugged her granddaughter.

As Sister helped Mo and Harvey get things unpacked in their new ranch-style house, she noticed some items were missing.

"Momma, where are all my old toys?" she questioned.

Mo answered, "Now Sister, aren't you getting a little old for toys? I sent them over to St. Peter's."

"Maybe so," she felt a bit sheepish, given that she was starting high school. Besides, her mother was thinking about the orphans so she realized she was being something of a brat. Under her breath, she whispered, "But they were *my* things."

Harvey ran out for some sandwiches. Mo was putting up dishes. Sister came into the kitchen where her mother was working.

"Momma, please tell me my dollhouse isn't at the orphanage!"

"Honey, I am sorry, I'm afraid it is."

Sister slammed shut her bedroom door and turned her radio up loud.

Such a display on Sister's part should have sent the old Mo right to the liquor store. It didn't. Mo Clark stopped drinking the day she left Memphis. Once settled in her new home, she became active in Immaculate Heart of Mary parish and began to attend Mass every morning. Apparently, to steady her resolve, Mo also stayed in correspondence by mail with a

Catholic priest in Nashville, Tennessee. He inspired her so much that Mo displayed the religious man's photograph atop her chest of drawers along with her rosary beads and a prayer book.

Mo picked Sister up each day at her new high school. She planted a beautiful rose garden and, as in Memphis, a bed of irises in every color and variety. After a long while of waiting for "Mo the drunk" to reappear, Sister and Harvey cautiously allowed themselves to enjoy the miracle.

One night Sister rode with Harvey to pick up some milk.

"Daddy," Sister began, "I'm glad you're not traveling so much."

Harvey glanced at his daughter and smiled. "Me, too, baby." He chuckled and shook his head. "Your mother seems to think so, too."

"Yeah," Sister said as she looked out the car window.

The Clarks quickly adjusted in their new home in Atlanta. Sister was doing well in school and made friends quickly.

"I can't wait to see your house, Nita," said Sister to her new friend, as she peered out the bus window. "Ya know, I've never been on a school bus before."

"Aren't you the snob!" replied Nita, jokingly.

"I am *not*! It's just that we don't live out here in the sticks, we're only five minutes away," explained Sister. "I'm in a carpool."

All too soon for Sister, the bus unloaded in the parking lot of Christ the King Cathedral and the kids scattered in different directions toward their homes.

"See you tomorrow," said one.

"Call me tonight," said another.

"It's not far," said Nita as they turned the corner.

After a few moments, they turned down the drive of a moderate home. Nita kicked the corner of the welcome mat and retrieved the door key.

"Is anything the matter?" Sister asked Nita.

Nita didn't appear to hear the question as she cautiously opened the door.

They went inside. "Is your mother home?" Sister asked.

"Take a seat in the kitchen," Nita sighed, nodding toward an open doorway. "I'll see."

The radio on the counter by the refrigerator was playing rock 'n roll music as Sister entered. Dirty dishes were stacked in the sink, but the rest of the kitchen was neat and tidy. A half-consumed cup of coffee sat on the table in front of her.

She heard voices. Nita said, "Mother! You promised. Come on, stand up."

Footsteps came down the stairs into the kitchen. Nita said, "This is Sister, Mother. She's the new girl from Memphis."

Holding the side of the counter, the mother said, "Memphis, you're from Memphis." She laughed and said, "I'll just bet you know Elvis Presley."

Nita moaned. "Mother, for goodness sakes, everyone from Memphis doesn't know him."

"No ma'am, I don't," said Sister, "but my grandmother saw him face to face once! Grandee's friend said she wished Elvis would give *her* a car. Guess what? Elvis heard her! And Elvis Presley gave Grandee's friend his brand new red Cadillac!"

Nita's mother stared at Sister blankly for a few seconds. "I like you, Memphis," she finally slurred.

"It's Sister, Mother, Sister Clark," corrected Nita. "Come on, Sister, let's go up to my room."

Nita glared at her mother and the two girls went upstairs.

They sat on the floor of Nita's bedroom and kicked off their uniform shoes. Sister dug her toes into the thick, soft white carpeting. Soon the two were lost in discussion about who liked whose music and what was going to top the music charts for that week.

Suddenly, Sister sniffed curiously. "I smell smoke!"

Nita responded immediately, "Good God, Mother!"

They raced down to the kitchen. The mother hurled a flaming potholder into the sink. It splashed in the dishwater and began to sizzle. A pan of cookies, burned almost to charcoal, flipped into the air and landed rolling all around on the floor. On the black and white tile floor, the cookies looked like misplaced checkers on a giant board.

"Damn it," muttered her mother. "I was only trying to make you and your Memphis friend happy."

"Just go rest, Mother. It's all right."

Sister stepped back so the lady could get by. She knew to say nothing.

"Nita, I'm sorry."

The embarrassed girl started to cry and then she stopped herself. "My mother is not feeling well, that's all."

"I know, it's all right. Really it is." She gingerly poked at a blackened cookie. "These look like cookies I would bake."

Nita didn't laugh.

"Come on, do you want to go back to your records?"

Nita stared at the cookies on the floor.

"Maybe I should go home since your mom's feeling so bad," Sister offered.

"Yeah, I guess so," Nita replied.

Twenty minutes later, Mo tooted the horn. Sister waved as she ran out to the car, "Nita, next time, my house!"

Nita didn't respond. She turned and went inside.

Mo asked, "What's wrong with your friend's mother?"

"Momma, I don't really know. Nita said not to worry. It happens all the time."

"That's a shame," said Mo.
"Thanks for coming, Momma."
"Let's stop for some ice cream," suggested Mo.
That night, Sister telephoned Nita.
"Thanks for calling, Sister," she said. "Everything's quiet. Mother's asleep."
The familiar knot twisted inside Sister's stomach.
"Next time" never came. Nita's father was transferred and moved his family to Chicago.

At the end of the year, Sister even summoned enough confidence in her mother to plan a party. "Spend the night" parties were all the rage. It was Harvey, not Mo, who complained about the event. While her mother thought her first slumber party was absolutely delightful, Sister's exhausted father complained, "Why are they called 'sleepovers' when you noisy girls stay awake the whole damn night?"

Just as any teenage girl would reply, Sister rolled her eyes and moaned, "Daddy, you just don't understand."

Mo laughed.

The parties flourished throughout high school. Junk food, cold drinks and hot chocolate, hair rollers, extra pillows, and a telephone were all that was necessary for such an event. Conversations about school, rock 'n roll music and gross and grisly ghost stories gradually evolved into chats about make-up, kissing, and college applications.

Grandee continued to remain in close touch with her family in Atlanta. For Christmas, for her summer vacations, for graduation, and for an occasional birthday, she would ride the Greyhound Bus all the way from Memphis to Atlanta. Every few miles, Grandee would take out a picture of Sister and check her watch.

Grandee always rode in the front seat of the bus, close to the driver. She wanted to keep her eye on his performance. As she exited the bus, whoever was making that particular run, would always tip his hat to her. She would then graciously nod and remark, "Thank you. You did a very nice job of driving us here."

"Thank you, ma'am."

She was always the very first passenger off the bus. And Sister was the first person in the crowd to greet the bus. They were still best friends, better than Grandee's friends in Memphis and better than Sister's friends at school. They would walk arm and arm as Sister attempted to repeat all at once everything she had already written throughout the months they had been apart.

"I've got a steady boyfriend, Grandee! I was saving that to tell you in person," announced Sister.

"He couldn't be good enough for you," she countered.

Sister was taken back. "Why, you haven't even met him yet, Grandee. How could you know?"

"See, I told you," she replied. "You're having your own doubts about the young man."

"I am not. He's *soooo* good looking."

Grandee was muttering "gracious sakes alive" when Harvey walked up with her things. "Are you girls ready to go home?"

"Indeed we are," said Grandee as she made sure her son-in-law had the tapestry suitcase and her old brown leather train case in hand.

On the way to their house, Sister explained, "Momma's at home. She thought you would want a snack as soon as we got you there."

"That's nice," replied Grandee. Her stomach tightened. Old fears die hard, even after three years.

Twenty minutes later, a sober Mo greeted them at the kitchen door. She was dressed in a fresh pressed house dress with navy pumps and stockings. Mo's blond, lightly-permed hair was secured behind her ears with two bobby pins, one on either side.

"Hello, Mother." There was only the usual stiffened hug between the mother and daughter. There was never touching except to quickly pat one another on the shoulder.

"Merry Christmas, Imogene," responded Grandee.

"And Merry Christmas to you. I've got apple pie for everyone," Mo said. "How about some with ice cream? Maybe melted cheese on top?"

"The ice cream sounds good. Thank you," answered Grandee.

Harvey was occupied with carrying his mother-in-law's things to the guestroom on the other side of the house. Sister helped her mother and quickly claimed the seat next to her grandmother.

"Now, Imogene, how are you?" Grandee asked her daughter.

"I'm fine, I suppose. Our little Sister is going off to college in the fall," her voice trailed off.

"That'll be good for her," said Grandee, eyeing Sister with a reassuring smile.

Their conversation touched on the weather, Christmas preparations, updates on various relatives and friends in Memphis. The bus trip had taken a toll on Grandee. She yawned a few times. Apologizing, she said, "I guess I'm getting old."

"No, you're not!" protested Sister.

Earlier when Harvey had questioned Grandee about the bus ride, she commented, "It was dreadful, simply dreadful. There were so many loud people traveling this time."

Then, as she ate her pie, her response to the identical query from Mo was, "It was, well, Imogene, all right, I suppose."

After more typical family conversation, again repeating much of what had already been written about in letters, the chatting slowed. Harvey was getting fidgety, and Mo was worn out from getting everything ready for her mother's visit.

Mo said, "I suggest we turn in. Tomorrow will be another busy day for us and, Mother, whether you'll admit it or not, I know you're tired."

"I suppose you're right," said Grandee.

Sister was delighted because she wanted her grandmother all to herself.

Sister followed Grandee to the guestroom. "The bus trip really did you in, did it?"

"Of course not," Grandee smiled. "It was perfectly wonderful, but now darling, tell me about your writing and the lovely nun, the English teacher? I want to hear all about the award your school paper won. I declare, I am proud of you," she said.

Sister hugged her best friend.

7

Harvey was again transferred. The move would take the Clarks away from Atlanta and to the company's home office in Birmingham. The move was scheduled some time after Sister's freshman year at the University of Alabama.

St. Pius High School sponsored an end of the year retreat for the graduating seniors. The retreat was held at the Ignatius Retreat House, located on the outskirts of Atlanta in a lovely wooded spot overlooking the Chattahoochee River. On a sunny May afternoon, Sister and her friend Betty Ann stood chatting by the turn-around of the Ignatius Retreat House. Next to Sister's overnight bag were freshly picked wild flowers for her mother. Mo would arrive any minute to pick up the two girls, and Sister couldn't wait to give her the bouquet.

"Sure feels good to be allowed to talk again," laughed Sister.

"Two days is two days too long for *you* to be quiet and reflective," teased Betty Ann.

Sister laughed and glanced at her watch. The other girls were long gone. As the minutes ticked by, she found herself growing tense. They waited.

"My watch must be wrong," Sister said. "What time is it?"

"4:30," answered her friend.

Mo was late. "Traffic," muttered Sister.

Every five minutes, she looked at her watch and repeated her question. And every five minutes, Betty Ann answered. Finally, getting somewhat irritated, her friend asked, "Why do you keep asking me the time? It doesn't matter."

Sister retorted, "No, it doesn't matter at all, Betty Ann!"

She didn't ask again.

Eventually, Mo rolled into the turn-around, narrowly missing the curb. Sister's chest caved in as her throat constricted. "Oh, my God, no." Sister recognized the half-closed left eye, the dropped corner of her mother's mouth, the disheveled hair, and, the dead give-a-way, the weaving automobile. The car slammed to a halt. Sister opened the door and peered at the woman in the driver's seat.

"Momma?"

Betty Ann pitched her overnight bag onto the back seat and hopped into the car. "Hello, Mrs. Clark. How are you today?"

"She's fine!" said Sister as she flung the wild flowers onto the gravel. "Want me to drive, Momma?"

"Just get in," her mother slurred.

She slammed her door. She was trapped.

Mo squealed off. Her tires shot gravel creating a wave behind the Clarks' car. The gravel pelted nearby green metal lawn chairs sounding like hail in a heavy thunderstorm. Sister shuddered.

"Way to go, Mrs. Clark," cheered Betty Ann.

Sister faked laughter.

She tried to catch a glimpse of her friend's face in the rearview mirror. Betty Ann seemed oblivious to Mo's condition.

"Mrs. Clark," inquired Betty Ann, "did Sister tell you about the hysterical remark Helen's mother made at the Gulf station?"

"Huh, what's that?" muttered Mo.

Taking her response as encouragement, Betty Ann began the story, "When we were on our way home from the beach"—Betty Ann screamed, "Mrs. Clark, look out!"

Mo jerked the steering wheel as the car ran off the road on the right side, and, as she turned, she went too far to the left and headed directly into the oncoming lane. A horn blared. Tires squealed.

"Momma!" yelled Sister.

Mo again swerved and they were safely back in the proper lane. She looked at Sister with a half-cocked eye and said, "No harm done, madam." On she drove.

"So as I was saying, Mrs. Clark, Helen and I simply *had* to go to the bathroom, and we all were dying for a Coke."

Mo mumbled, "You gals want a Coke?"

"No, Momma! Betty Ann is talking about our trip to Florida."

"Well, *I* want a damn Coke!" Mo bit back.

Sister sat in silence. Mo drove on.

"Anyway, Mrs. Murray pulled into a Gulf station and, you know Mrs. Murray, so when she said 'hurry,' we did." Betty Ann giggled as she recounted the scene. "So, we all got back in the car, passed around the chips and drinks while Mrs. Murray talked with the man who was cleaning the windshield. Mrs. Murray rolled down her window and stuck her head out. She cleared her throat and shouted in that deep commanding voice of hers, 'When you are done with the windshield, young man, you can wipe my rear!'"

"We were on the floor laughing. And when she realized what she had said, Mrs. Murray laughed even harder!" Sister relaxed with the memory.

Mo remarked, "I'm still thirsty."

"Whoops, Mrs. Clark, you missed my driveway."

Mo screeched backwards and roared up the hill to the Putnams' house.

"Oh, Mother's car isn't here," said Betty Ann.

Sister breathed a sigh of relief. She certainly did not want Mrs. Putnam to see her mother in this state.

"So," said Mo, "What's the story about Jo Murray? Did she want a Coke?"

Sister tensed up. "Just forget it Momma."

Betty Ann was already out of the Clark's car. She said, "I'm sure Mother left a key under the mat for me. Thank you, Mrs. Clark, I really appreciate the ride." She reached for her bag and closed the door. "Call me, Sister."

"Sure."

Sister's face was red as Mo backed down the driveway. *How could you, Momma?* she thought. Sister was even mad at God. *I was so close to You this morning as I walked in those woods.* She thought about her joy when she picked the flowers. Tiny blossoms of purple and yellow. A pang of regret hit her in the stomach as she recalled pitching the innocent blooms on the gravel drive.

Mo stomped her foot as she clumsily tried to find the brake. Too late. The car ran over a curb. Sister froze as she grabbed the dashboard to brace herself.

"Momma, I'd *really* like to drive," she volunteered.

"Chillun should be seen, not heard," mumbled Mo as she backed up. With a lunge and a bump they were off once more.

Sister took a breath. "Lord, help us." Just that morning at the retreat, she had prayed with such love for her mother. Now her prayers were for self-preservation. Again, Mo slammed on the brakes. They were directly under a red light, stopped in the dead center of the intersection.

Horns honked.

"Damn rude drivers," Mo growled.

"Momma."

"Quiet, I'm trying to concentrate."

"That's not a street!" Sister screamed. The car sideswiped a mailbox and went down an embankment. They came to another stop. "What the hell?" Mo spit.

Sister didn't care if either she or Mo were hurt. She was worried about whether or not the car could move. Escape. They had to get out of there. Mo stomped the accelerator. Off they went. Sister looked back—they left skid marks thirty feet long. Someone's once-manicured lawn looked as if a train had run through it. Branches from a bank of soft pink azalea bushes clung to the underside of the Clark's car.

Finally home, Sister went to her bedroom. She slammed the door. And, throwing herself across her bed, she wept. If Mo passed out somewhere, her daughter didn't bother to check.

The next morning, Sister got out of bed and went into the kitchen. Her mother stood at the sink. She had cut some flowers and was arranging them in an assortment of vases. The containers were lined up across the kitchen counter top. Sister knew her mother's routine. She would put one arrangement on the breakfast table; another one, probably the roses with honeysuckle, in the den; a third in the living room on the table at the end of the sofa, and there would be one in Sister's bedroom.

"Damn the flowers," Sister hissed under her breath. *At least, I'll be going to the Univeristy of Alabama in the fall,* she thought with relief.

Mo turned from the sink and smiled at her daughter. "Good morning, honey."

Sister turned and went outside to sit in the sun.

Sister's four years at the University of Alabama were glorious. She loved every minute she was there. She was a good student and soon joined a sorority. Interesting classes, fraternity parties, and college football games dominated Sister's life. Then she met Jack Sanford. Sister was introduced to Jack at a pledge swap. Much to the dismay of her "big sister" who thought the two of them would be a perfect match, Sister and Jack didn't hit it off. She thought him rude; he saw her as stuck-up. Fate had a different plan. For the next few months, they ran into one another at every turn. Each time, Sister couldn't help but notice that Jack always had a cute coed at his side. Every one of those girls seemed charmed by the young man.

Humm, thought Sister, *I must have overlooked something in this boy.*

So when Jack asked her out in the spring, she jumped at the chance. "Well, maybe," she responded, "although I do have another date for Saturday. I'll see if I can get out of it."

She did. She never dated another boy.

Grandee was kept current on Jack, on events in the sorority, especially about Sister's initiation as a full-fledged member, and about any other good news concerning her success in college. She wrote to Grandee about the football games, about Jack's fraternity parties, and often inquired about her grandmother's doings in Memphis. At the same time, in her weekly letters, Sister never mentioned failing chemistry the first time around. Although, Grandee might have thought it clever that she and a classmate managed to improve their chemistry grades the second term by giving a bottle of bourbon to a student lab assistant for his help with their experiments.

It worked; they both passed.

Nonetheless, if whatever was happening might have caused her grandmother a moment's worry, Sister simply chose to leave it out of her letters. She believed that Grandee deserved *not* to hear bad news. After all, ignoring a bad situation had become a family tradition.

"Are we the only students left in Tuscaloosa?" Sister jokingly asked her ride as she loaded her things into the trunk of his car. Two days before she had kissed Jack goodbye for the summer. Because of the pressure of academic concerns going on with both of them, their quick pizza together wasn't much of a memory for the young couple.

The past ten days had been a foggy nightmare of staying up all night to cram for each final, of nervously opening the light blue test booklet, and two hours later, breathing a sigh of relief at its completion. Sister would walk back to her dorm and immediately return to her self-imposed study regime. Final exams had been a bleak time of constant tension, of too little real food, too much caffeine, and absolutely no recreation.

As she watched out the car window, the realization of the summer without her new boyfriend depressed her, still the thoughts of seeing her friends, spending time with her parents, and just being in her own home without the stress of college perked her up. And there was the Clark's upcoming move to Birmingham to consider. After this summer, the distance from Tuscaloosa to Atlanta would be cut to the one-hour-drive between Tuscaloosa and Birmingham. Sister drifted off to sleep.

She retrieved her two suitcases and her hanging clothes from the boy's car. She waved goodbye as he pulled off. "Thanks again, I don't know what I'd done if you hadn't been leaving today!"

Sister went inside dropping her things in the breakfast nook. "Momma! Daddy, I'm home!"

Mo came into the kitchen from the den. "I was getting worried," she said.

"I'm sorry, the guy ran late, and we did stop a couple of times," said Sister.

"I hate that you drove in the dark," answered Mo.

"I know," Sister said. "Where's Daddy?"

"I don't remember. Florida, I think."

Sister was disappointed. This wasn't the welcome home she'd predicted.

"Did you eat?" inquired her mother.

"Oh, Momma, again I'm sorry. I'm afraid we did stop for a hamburger. But if you want me to have something, I will."

"Forget it," said Mo. "It doesn't matter."

Sister looked at her mother for a long moment. She couldn't think of much else besides rest. "Momma, I am nearly dead, do you mind if I go on to bed?"

Mo shrugged her shoulders and said, "Suit yourself."

"Thanks, Momma. Good night."

As she brushed her teeth, Sister recalled the incident after the retreat and wondered if the drinking had begun. She called an immediate halt to her thinking telling herself that she was just in a bad mood. "Momma's mad because we were late and that I didn't want dinner," she rationalized. As soon as she pulled her soft familiar quilt up around her neck, the young woman was sound asleep.

It was almost lunchtime the next day when she awakened. She had hardly moved during the night. Getting out of bed, Sister rummaged in her closet and found her favorite old plaid flannel bathrobe. She stuck her feet in comfy terry-cloth slippers and walked into the kitchen. Mo was reading the paper. A cigarette was perched on the lip of her glass ashtray.

"Good morning, Sleeping Beauty," she said. "I'm on my third cup of coffee. Have some."

"No thanks, I may be a college girl, but I still don't drink coffee," replied Sister as she opened the refrigerator and poured some orange juice into a jelly glass decorated with little red cherries.

Mo stood up. When Sister saw her mother's frame in the morning light, her eyes grew wide. "Momma, have you lost some weight?"

"No, I probably need to though."

"You sure look like you already have," Sister said, taking a bite out of a donut. "I'm as fat as a pig!"

"Hmmmm," mumbled Mo.

"I sure feel better this morning. It's nice to be home," Sister said glancing about the kitchen. Mo had lost weight. Even her face appeared drawn, and her wrinkles were more evident that before. The Clarks' house was messy. There was little food in the refrigerator and no June flowers deco-rated the tabletops. Later on when she walked outside, Sister noticed that weeds were beginning to take over her mother's iris bed.

"Momma, when is Daddy coming home?"

"Soon, I suppose. He knows you're here."

Sister showered and wrote a letter to Jack. She lost herself in missing him and inquiring about his summer job. *Only 64 days until I'm back for Rush!* she wrote for herself as much as for him. *Is there any chance you could come for a visit?* she asked assuring herself that her mother would rally for that event. Momma would do that for her, wouldn't she?

Once back in Tuscaloosa, she was busy with Jack, sorority Rush Week, and with her studies; so Sister simply ignored the obvious. Besides, the Clarks' move to Birmingham would be completed in a week or two. Momma would rally.

In the late summer of 1964, the Clarks moved from Atlanta to Birmingham. It would be the final undoing of Mo. She so loathed her new surroundings that she abandoned all resolve for sobriety. She didn't go to church or work in the garden

Harvey put in for her. She refused to respond to people who reached out to her. Mo wouldn't answer the telephone.

Harvey had gone back to traveling full time. The reality of that situation became profoundly real to Sister on September 17. It was her daddy's birthday, and she decided to take Jack to Birmingham to her parent's new house to surprise him. After all, Jack had seen her mother only once and her father on two occasions.

As Sister and Jack drove up the hill on Heritage Circle, she noticed the house was dark. "Darn, they must be out to dinner!" she said to Jack, hoping to cover her own fears.

After pulling into the garage, Sister got out of Jack's car. She walked over to the door and inserted her key into the lock. The door swung opened. Sister suggested Jack stay downstairs in the den.

She made her way up the darkened steps and felt for the light switch. She walked through the kitchen and into the living room. She found Mo passed out on the sofa. A cigarette had fallen out of the ashtray. It had rolled and burned a black spot in the table as it went out. Daddy was nowhere to be found.

Sister said nothing. She scrawled a note and left it on the kitchen table.

It was a week before Sister heard from either of her parents. It was her father who called. He said, "Hello, honey, I'm so sorry I missed your visit." He'd been out of town, somewhere in Florida, she thought she heard him say. He never mentioned Mo, not once.

Six months later, Jack asked Sister if she would marry him after graduation. She said yes. Throughout their junior and senior years, she thought of little else but her boyfriend and the future they would share.

Grandee was only mildly pleased that Sister had fallen in love. She liked Jack enough when they met during the holidays the next year, but Sister could see her grandmother was fairly reserved about him.

"Oh, he's nice, I suppose," she'd finally responded to Sister's questioning regarding Jack.

Grandee had never been big on sharing her only granddaughter with anyone, but, as she was eventually to concede, "I'm happy, if my little darling is happy."

To her credit, Mo Clark once again pulled herself together valiantly to plan a lovely wedding for her only child. She worked for months on it. That suited Sister fine. She was overwhelmed with school, with graduation and too much in love with Jack to worry about the details of her wedding.

All throughout the spring of 1967, Mo was preoccupied with decisions about flowers for the church and food for the reception along with choices of music and the listing of wedding gifts as they started to arrive. Like the phoenix, Mo came soaring back from the ashes.

One Saturday in June, a week before they were to marry, Jack and Sister had an evening out. He hardly spoke to her during the entire evening they were together; and when he did, Jack snapped at his bride-to-be. On the way home from a movie that neither one of them watched, Sister tried to tease him out of his mood. "What's the matter?" she joked. "Are you gettin' cold feet about becoming my husband?"

Jack pulled into the Clarks' driveway and stopped the car so suddenly they both lunged forward. He blurted out, "I've got to go over there, Sister. Damn, I didn't want to tell you until after the wedding." He shook his head sadly. "I'm so sorry."

"Sorry about what?" Sister asked, turning to him and resting a hand on his shoulder.

Tears welled up in his eyes as Jack said, "I got my orders today," he hesitated.

"And?"

He said, "I'm going to Vietnam."

Sister went numb. She turned away mutely before turning back to him. "When?" she asked.

"October."

She stammered, "Couldn't there be some mistake?"

"Not a chance," he countered. "When I opened the packet, a book fell out. It was 'Familiar Vietnamese Phrases.'" That almost made the two of them laugh. Almost, but not quite.

Jack's orders being issued a week to the day before her daughter's wedding had been about the last straw for Mo.

On the afternoon of the wedding rehearsal, the bride drove out to the airport to pick up her beloved Grandee. Mo ran her own last minute errands; unfortunately, they included a stop by the liquor store.

Mo slept through the rehearsal, through the party that followed, and until the next morning. Sister and Jack, Harvey, Grandee, and the Sinclair relatives from Memphis, as their custom dictated, made the best of things. They had some practice through the years.

"I know you must be thrilled that your wedding day is finally here, dear," chirped one of the cousins.

"Tomorrow, oh my! Sister, you're going to make a lovely bride," remarked another.

"Oh, I'm very excited. Thank you so much for coming," responded Sister politely.

"Sorry you have to turn around and go to Vietnam, son," said a Sanford family member, shaking his head as he patted Jack on the back.

"Don't worry, sir, your country will be in good hands," answered Jack, trying to lighten the moment for everyone's sake.

"Your poor Imogene," whispered a kind relative to Grandee.

Grandee stood there stoically, looking exhausted.

Uncle Will hugged Sarah and said, "I know your daughter is simply worn out from all her preparations, dear."

Sister overheard the conversation and kissed each of the Sinclairs on their cheeks, "Indeed, she is. I'm certain Momma will feel better in the morning.

The next morning, it was as if nothing had happened.

Harvey arrived at St. Francis Catholic Church with Mo and Grandee. He got the two of them situated temporarily in some comfortable chairs and congratulated himself that things hadn't gotten any worse. Mo had managed to don her pink mother of the bride dress and matching shoes. Her hat wobbled atop her head like the plate a juggler spins on a stick. In her typical form, Mo shook her way though the wedding and reception that followed.

Sister drove herself home from the airport. Jack's devastated parents wanted her to ride with them. She wouldn't. She couldn't. Instead Sister got into Jack's car and screamed and wept. It was thirty minutes before she could see to drive out of the airport parking deck.

Sister turned on the car radio. She turned it off. The bride who had dreamed about her wedding for two and a half years did not want to hear "My Girl." If she heard the words, "I've got sunshine on a cloudy day," she'd surely collapse.

As she pulled into Harvey's space in the garage, she felt sick. Jack was going to war in Southeast Asia, and she was going into battle on Heritage Circle.

Sister used the last of her Kleenex and went inside. "Momma?"

As usual, there was no reply. Her mother had made no attempt to go to the airport with them. Had she even mentioned to her parents Jack's actual day to leave? Maybe not. She never wanted to say the day and time out loud and make it real.

"Oh, it's you!" said Mo. "I thought it was your father."

"Nope, it's just me."

"Where's Jack?" her mother asked.

"Vietnam."

"Honey, I am sorry. I, I would have gone, but..." Mo's voice trailed off.

"It's okay, Momma." Sister started up the steps. Mo followed.

"Your father went, but, of course you know that," began Mo.

Sister spun around. She raised her voice and said, "Yes, and I was born while he was in Germany. And I was six months old before he saw me. And I had colic all those months! I know Momma!" Immediately, Sister wished she could swallow her words. "Please forget what I said, Momma."

"T'weren't much fun," Mo said absently.

"At least I'm not pregnant like you were," commented Sister.

"Thank God for small favors," Mo muttered. She gazed at the floor a moment, silent. Her mother seemed lost in thought. Mo shook her head, pursed her lips and said, "Damn Roosevelt and damn that idiot Johnson, too."

8

Jack was gone every minute of his year-long tour in the Adjutant General Corps. The major enemy he had to fight was time.

Sister spent their year apart working as a reporter for the *Birmingham News*, looking forward to their R&R in Hawaii for their first wedding anniversary and counting the hours until October 5, 1968 when she and Jack could begin their lives.

During the long, lonely year, Sister also had to deal with Mo. One night Harvey called his daughter at the apartment she shared with three girlfriends. "Honey, can you come over here," he asked. "We've got a mess."

A few minutes later at her parent's house, Harvey met her at the door. "Look at this," he said shaking his head. He handed his daughter a note. It was her mother's hand writing. *Harvey, go to the store, I need cigarettes. And get the gun. Do it now. Mo.*

Sister looked up from the scrawled note. "Daddy! What gun? What is she talking about?"

Harvey explained that the gun was one that Sarah had kept for protection. Several months before, she had given it to him to keep because it worried her more to have it around.

"You're not going to give Momma a gun, are you?" Sister asked in stunned surprise.

"No! Of course not," he said irritably. "It's just that I don't know what to do. Is she thinking about killing herself?"

"Good Lord, Daddy," said Sister, "you can't pay attention to her crazy ramblings."

Upstairs they could hear Mo as she stumbled around her room. She was mumbling obscenities. Sister looked upwards at the sound and took a deep breath. She tried to be compassionate for her father's sake. "Daddy, I'm sorry about all of this. Please, just make certain the gun is safely stored in your lock box and try to talk with Momma when she's sober."

October 5 came at last and Jack landed at the Birmingham airport. His happy family was there in full force to welcome him home. Jack was grinning as he ran off the airplane. As he hurried through the terminal door, the thin, uniformed soldier threw down his duffle bag and held wide his arms.

"Go see your baby boy!" urged Sister as she pushed her mother-in-law toward the son she hadn't seen in an entire year. Mary ran into Jack's widespread arms. "Oh, you're soooo beautiful!" she exclaimed. He hugged her and reached for his dad who was weeping with joy.

Jack then turned to Sister. He swept up his bride and she melted into his embrace. Sister wouldn't let go of her husband for days.

In November, Grandee decided to plan a "Welcome Home" dinner party for her new grandson-in-law. She wanted to celebrate the young couple's happy reunion and Jack's military service. She invited the Sanfords to Memphis for a long weekend. Up Grandee's sleeve was a unique tribute, one that she had worked out with the help of some of her connections at city hall.

The night of her dinner party, Grandee, looking for all the world like a family matriarch, began the festivities with a toast. She tapped her glass and said, "I want to welcome all of you here tonight. I especially want to welcome our guest of honor, Lt. Jack Sanford."

Everyone stood and applauded.

Soon dinner was served and the gathering of family and friends subsided into warm conversation. Just before the dessert was served, Grandee rose from her place at the head of the table and again called for attention. "At this time, I would like to honor Sister's fine young man, Jack."

Jack stood. He looked questioningly toward Sister.

She shrugged her shoulders.

"Jack," continued Grandee, "We, along with the entire city of Memphis, want to thank you for your service to our country. We welcome you home."

Everyone clapped as Grandee presented Lt. Jack Sanford with the key to the city of Memphis. Jack graciously thanked everyone. "And in conclusion, I want to say a special word of thanks to Sister's beloved grandmother, Sarah Sinclair," he said indicating the award. "I certainly never expected such a tribute. And even more so," Jack continued, "I thank you, Grandee, for the gift of your granddaughter."

Later as the gathering dispersed, Sister found her grandmother. "Jack loved the surprise, Grandee," said Sister. "It was wonderful. I'm so proud of you."

"It was nothing, dear," said Grandee.

The next busy years in Birmingham went by in fast frames of jobs for Sister and Jack, two apartments, a first house and, at last, three babies. Sister and Jack Sanford first shared their hearts with a daughter, Sarah Elizabeth or "Eliza," in 1971. A year later, their first son, William, was born; and in 1976, came a second son, Edward. Their three children completed the Sanford's family and gave immeasurable joy to Sister and to Jack, and most assuredly, to four justifiably proud grandparents, and, of course, to Grandee.

Sister had yearned for a happy family for her whole life. So much so, she created her own. The Sanford family included three children, a daddy who stayed in town, and a mother who never napped.

Sister stood smiling at her two older children who were at play in the den of the Sanford's new home. Just after Edward was born in 1976, Jack and Sister had purchased the larger house. Located at the top of a steep driveway in the Birmingham suburb of Vestavia Hills, the home was an L-shaped ranch house with a big kitchen on the front. Sister thought she had died and gone to heaven. She loved her house, she loved her three children, and she loved Jack.

Eliza and William had their toys spread from one end of the house to the other. Edward was propped up in his infant seat safely away from his very active siblings. He cooed happily. Edward had recently found his toes and was completely captivated by the discovery.

Clutching a plastic action figure, William bargained, "I'll make my man stop fighting your dumb Strawberry Shortcake doll, if you give me a piece of that cake."

Eliza's brown eyes flashed. Holding a potholder, she stood between William and her Easy Bake Oven. The aroma of her chocolate cake baking had tempted her younger brother more than he could stand. "Oh pleeese," he begged.

Her brother had tricked her before. "I know you, Weyum," she fussed. "You'll promise, then after you eat the cake, you'll forget!"

Sister stifled her laughter at the exchange. Edward kicked gleefully as Sister picked him up. "Do you want some of your big sister's baking, too, precious boy?" she offered.

The round pink baby gurgled.

"Eliza," Sister remarked, "you better get busy. You'll soon have two brothers who love your pastries." The mother took the top off the black iron skillet and stirred the dinner for that night. With three children to care for, she was definitely going with easy-to-prepare-foods. They were having pot roast for the first time. She had peeled and cut the onions, carrots, and potatoes while Edward took his morning nap and Eliza and William were in kindergarten.

The roast's scent filled the room. "Jack should be delighted," she beamed. He had cooked on the grill for the family the night before and brought home Chinese food another night that week. She lamented, "This poor man is due a nice dinner that he didn't have to cook for himself."

She arranged the plates and utensils on the table.

Odd that I haven't thought about the chuck cut before now, she thought. *Momma used to cook it all the time.*

Sister cuddled Edward close to her heart. She felt so content, so safe. Dinner simmered. Sister made certain her roast didn't burn.

On Christmas afternoon, the Sanfords pulled into Harvey and Mo's driveway. Eliza and William raced out of the car to see who could ring the doorbell first.

Faster this time, William said, "I gotta go help Daddy now, but I'll be right back." The little boy ran back to his father unloading presents from the car.

As Sister carried Edward inside, her father whispered, "Your mother is all right today."

She wanted to respond with some caustic remark, but as soon as she saw Grandee, her heart softened. "Grandee!" Sister said running to where she was seated. "You're here! I am so glad to see you. How are you feeling?"

"Why, I'm just fine, of course" said the grandmother, beaming at her granddaughter. She pushed the soft blue blanket away from Edward's face and said, "I understand there's someone here I should meet."

Sister grinned. "This is Edward. Oh, Grandee, isn't he adorable?"

She quickly inspected Edward and declared, "I see that this one is just as darling as my other two."

Like water dousing a warm, roaring fire, Mo strode from the kitchen and through the dining room to stand in front of Grandee and Sister. "I guess Harvey told you that the stupid power went off this morning," she growled. "I don't know when we'll be able to eat the damn dinner."

"Merry Christmas, Mo!" Jack said as he pushed open the door with an armful of gifts. William followed behind him carrying his stack.

Sister rose quickly to help her husband. "Here, please put everything around Momma's Christmas tree."

O Come, All Ye Faithful was playing on the stereo.

After taking time to arrange the gifts, Sister turned back to Mo. "Momma, can I help you do something?"

"No, you'd just be in the way," she responded. "Besides, you have enough to do with the baby," Mo said, nodding toward the bundle in Grandee's arms. Mo turned on her heels and went back to the kitchen.

Just then began, "Hark the Herald Angels Sing…"

"Daddy, I thought you said Momma was all right?"

Harvey replied, "I said all right, not pleasant."

Jack began playing with the children as Sister, Grandee, and Harvey chatted. Some minutes had passed when Mo made her second entrance. "Since dinner will be late thanks to *wonderful* Alabama Power, I think we should let the children open their little things."

"Fair enough," agreed Jack.

Harvey disappeared and returned carrying a huge box with a bright green ribbon tied around it. "Let's see," teased the grandfather. "It says, 'to William from Santa.' Does anybody in this room know a boy named William?"

William sprang to his feet and tore into the wrapping. "It's me, PaPaw, I'm named William!" Strips of Christmas paper, ribbon, packaging and pieces of cardboard flew all around the Clarks' living room. The frenzied boy tried to climb inside what remained of the big box as he shrieked. One by one, he retrieved the treasures it held.

As the last of the box's contents were discovered, Mo leaned down to Eliza. "Eliza, I think I just heard something coming from upstairs. Can you hear anything?"

Eliza stood straight and cocked her head as though to listen. "Do you think it could be Santa?"

"It might just be. Why don't we go upstairs and both take a good look around?" Mo took Eliza by the hand as they walked up the steps.

After a curious glance to Jack, Sister passed her husband the baby and followed the unlikely pair. The trio crept up the stairs. As they reached the top, Mo pushed a bedroom door wide.

Sister's mouth dropped open.

Eliza squealed, "Look, oh look how beautiful it is!" She sat cross-legged as she began to inspect every inch of the white, two-storied dollhouse with dark green shutters. Each of the four rooms was filled with furniture and someone had placed a tiny, decorated Christmas tree right in the middle of the living room floor. There was a doll family, too, a family with a father, a mother, a little girl, a little boy, and a baby brother.

Mo beamed with pride.

"Momma...," Sister began.

Mo turned to her daughter. "Go ahead," she said, "get down and play with the dollhouse if you feel like it."

Grandee peeked into the room and smiled.

Sadly, Mo generally spent most of her time mired in the haze of drunkenness broken only by an occasional morning spent with the three grandchildren whom she didn't know exactly how to love.

Harvey, who retired after fifty years with the same company, discovered golf. He visited his grandchildren and became a loyal fan of whatever any one of them was doing. For five years, Papaw never missed a soccer game.

Mo's cousin Howard Sinclair died suddenly of a heart attack. Jack remained at home with the children so Sister could travel to Memphis with Mo and Harvey.

Sister and Grandee's niece Annette, were standing together at a funeral home in Memphis. Looking up from the casket, Annette asked Sister if Grandee was terribly upset when she heard the news of Howard's death. "I know how hysterically she reacts when people die."

Sister was stunned. "My Grandee, hysterical?" That was not a possibility. Grandee was clearly the calmest, most reserved and dignified person one could imagine. Proud and efficient, she had never exhibited an emotional response to anything Sister could recall. Bewildered, Sister asked, "Hysterical? No, she only said she wished she'd died instead of Howard." Sister reminded Annette that Grandee was ninety-something, which was another well-kept secret at that time, and Howard was only seventy years old. "Howard was a young man in his prime to Grandee's way of thinking, Annette," replied Sister. "She considered Howard's premature death as an unfortunate waste of his youth."

"Oh, I see," replied Annette skeptically. The two sat down to talk. The subject of Sister's grandfather came up.

Initially, Annette began to share things regarding the late Eugene W. Sinclair that Sister had heard only in bits and pieces. Annette, who was a teenager when her uncle died, said the man was absolutely charming, a wonderful real estate salesman, and was apparently revered by everyone in the Sinclair family and, in kind, by the Memphis community as a whole. "Everyone loved Eugene, and Eugene returned that love," Annette said. "This was especially true of Grandee. Uncle Eugene simply worshipped Sarah and your mother as well, his precious princess, the very spoiled Imogene." Annette smiled sadly.

While she spoke, it became abundantly clear to Sister that her grandfather had been a delightful man, a caring and engaging friend to all who knew him. It was information to which she had never been privy. A very happy and devoted husband and father was Eugene Sinclair.

"It was such a tragedy that he killed himself," Annette said, shaking her head slowly.

"What?!" Sister asked, looking intently at Annette. "Suicide? I thought my grandfather died in a car wreck?"

"Oh, yes, you're right, there was a car accident, a terrible one, in fact. When I saw Uncle Eugene, he was in enormous pain. He hardly looked like himself."

Sister stared in disbelief.

Annette continued, "The doctor said he never would have recovered. And the poor dear, Uncle Eugene was left partially paralyzed."

Sister listened.

"Then a few days after they brought him home, he found the revolver and shot himself in the head." She paused, "It came as a terrible shock to everyone."

Dizzy, Sister looked down at the floor. "A terrible shock," Sister repeated with a deep sign.

"Mr. Sinclair" was what Grandee preferred to call her husband on the very rare occasions she chose to speak of him. Reflecting back, Sister could hardly remember more than two or three times that she heard her grandmother say his name. Grandee always managed to change the subject anytime someone else mentioned Eugene Sinclair in a conversation. Sister, at age ten or so, was searching for something in Grandee's top bureau drawer. She stumbled upon a beautiful, illustrated book, *An Old Sweetheart of Mine* by James Whitcomb Riley.

Sister gently leafed through the pages of what obviously was a very special and cherished book. She began to notice what appeared to have been personal messages written in the margins throughout the book's printed verse. Each word was completely rubbed clean by an eraser. The paper, rubbed lighter in those spots, still bore the scars of what was once there. Not a syllable could be read.

"Grandee, I love this book!" said Sister, as she sat on the side of her grandmother's daybed one lazy Saturday afternoon in her grandmother's apartment. Turning the pages, she observed, "Look, something was written on this page, and here, too. Grandee, I believe someone has erased a bunch of stuff!"

Her grandmother sat quietly and sewed.

"Who do you think wrote in your book, Grandee? Can't you see? Someone has rubbed out all the words." Sister pleaded for her response.

Grandee answered, "Open the candy drawer. Why don't you pick out a treat for yourself, little darling?"

That was the end of that.

Some weeks after the funeral, Sister studied the lone photograph of her grandmother on her own dining room wall. In profile, Sarah's soft hair is twisted up to reveal her long graceful neck. On her right pinkie finger is a diamond dinner ring. A lace and satin blouse caress her shoulder. "How do you do, Sarah!" Sister whispered.

Throughout the years, some in the family had lovingly teased her as they referred to the old photo as "the glamour girl shot." Grandee firmly dismissed any such remarks with, "Paashaw. Don't talk such foolishness."

A few weeks later, Grandee was visiting at Sister's home. The two of them were chatting over coffee in the kitchen. Sister poured them each a second cup and asked, "Grandee, please tell me about when my grandfather died?"

First, there was a prolonged silence. Then the lady, the sturdy and valiant woman, the grandmother who crafted much of what was happy about Sister's childhood, who made the beautiful doll clothes, who fed her and took away so much pain, who helped her do well in school and later wrote each week for twenty-five years, who rescued her dollhouse and called out her spelling words and sold magazine subscriptions for her at the auditorium so she wouldn't have to take time from her studies; the grandmother who loved her more than anyone on earth, turned her eyes away.

Then Grandee lied.

She said firmly, "Mr. Sinclair died in a car wreck."

Sister took a deep breath. "Grandee, do you think it's possible that my grandfather's death could be the reason Momma drinks?"

Grandee's words felt to Sister like a rush of freezing water. The only thing she permitted herself to say was, "No, darling, your mother, poor little Imogene, was much more upset about the sorority she pledged."

"What?" stammered Sister.

"Oh, she wanted to pledge Chi Omega, but instead the Kappa Deltas selected her."

Silence.

Grandee would say nothing more.

9

Grandee turned ninety-five in November of 1984. Sister drove over to Birmingham from Atlanta where she and Jack had moved in 1982. Sister always made a concerted effort to celebrate the special day. As the two of them sat in Denny's for her grandmother's favorite pancake and scrambled egg brunch, Grandee said, "It's a shame Imogene wasn't feeling well enough to join us."

"I know," sighed Sister.

While they waited for their food, Grandee opened her cards and presents. She always loved greeting cards.

"I saved the best for last," she said as she carefully opened the gifts and messages from each of her great grandchildren who had begrudgingly remained in Atlanta for school that day. Eliza, age thirteen, sent a bouquet of fall flowers. She opened an envelope from William, age twelve. He had spent more than an hour writing her a letter in which he explained, in great detail, his team's soccer victory the previous Saturday. "Happy Birthday, Grandee," he penned. "I'll score a goal just for you next week."

Edward, age eight, had drawn a cake with the sixty candles, saying he'd run out of room for the rest of the candles. Grandee said, "Edward's makes me younger, and that's just wonderful."

Grandee had moved from Memphis to Birmingham a few years prior to be closer to Imogene and Harvey and to Sister, Jack, and her great grandchildren. The truth was she believed that with a little encouragement Mo might be able to "behave herself" just as she had for those happy years in Atlanta. Within a month, Grandee had arranged to live in a retirement home.

Sister came over from Atlanta to visit as often as she could, but it wasn't nearly enough for either of them. Harvey became his mother-in-law's most consistent visitor. Mo would drop by on occasion to bring flowers.

"Mother, how you be?" she would say as she poked her head in the door of the apartment.

"All right, I suppose," replied Grandee. "How are *you*?"

Mo didn't answer. Hands trembling, she tried to put a vase of roses on the table near her mother. The water spilled all onto the tabletop. "Damn."

Mo began dabbing at the water with a nearby napkin.

Grandee said, "Don't worry, I'll take care of that for you."

"Okay, gotta run."

"Your flowers are so pretty. Thank you, Imogene," said Grandee, as the door closed behind her daughter.

As fast as Mo had come, Mo was gone.

Grandee wrote to Sister and her family to thank them for their "birthday thoughts." Three months later, her grandmother made the decision to die. Grandee waited for Sister to go out of the country. She was in Mexico on a vacation with Jack to celebrate her fortieth birthday. Jack teased her at a sight of some Mayan ruins saying, "See, honey, I told you we would discover something older than you in this place." She kicked at her husband playfully and made him take a picture of her with the ancient temple in the background.

Later, maybe an hour drive from Cancun, the Sanfords came upon an almost-deserted, palm-framed lagoon. As they watched with a handful of people, a native scaled to the top of a coconut tree to gather its fruit. Sister and Jack walked on the beach with the ocean lapping at their feet. "Doesn't get much better than this," Jack said as he squeezed close his wife.

Completely relaxed, the couple drank in the tropical panorama of the salt white sand and turquoise water. Sister reached for the camera to try to capture the flavor of the breathtaking scenery. As she focused the lens, a double rainbow streaked across the brilliant blue sky.

Sister Sanford burst into tears.

Jack was totally bewildered. "What on earth is wrong? Why are you crying?"

"I am simply overwhelmingly happy," beamed Sister. "I don't know the reason, but something wonderful has happened. I can feel it."

Their phone was ringing as the Sanfords came in from the airport.

Sister grabbed it. "Hello."

His voice cracking, her father blurted out, "Grandee's dead!"

Sister went limp as her father's broken voice came over the phone. "They found her in bed," he continued. Harvey explained that when she hadn't gone to her meals in the retirement home, the ladies she usually ate with got worried. A staff member went to check on her. "They told me Mrs. Sinclair went to bed and never woke up," his voice trailed off.

"Poor, poor Grandee," cried Sister.

"Baby, no one even knows what happened because she wasn't found for so long. We can't even figure out exactly when she died."

Sister said, "Daddy, I think I know," smiling as she thought back on the double rainbow.

Hanging up the phone a few minutes later, Sister walked around her house. She should unpack and repack. They'd fly to Memphis. There'd be a service to plan. She swallowed hard.

She wasn't thinking very clearly. The children would be getting off the school bus any minute. She'd have to tell them their great grandmother had passed away. Sister paced around in circles. Her house, usually bright with color and music, seemed as cold and quiet as a cave. She wanted to cry.

Sister sat gazing at the empty hole where her Grandee would be buried. She turned her eyes away from the spot. Jack and the children huddled against the brutal wind as they sat under the tent on cold metal chairs. Rumpled green carpet bunched under their feet.

Sister recalled a pledge she had made to her grandmother. "You must promise me now that you won't cry at my graveside service," insisted Grandee.

"What? You'll never die, Grandee!" she had countered.

Grandee wasn't pleased. Her granddaughter gave in.

Sister couldn't remember exactly when that conversation took place; she wished she could forget it did. Sister blinked away a tear. She squeezed someone's hand; whose, she couldn't recall. Sister remembered squeezing and trying to take in air. Her eyes were drawn again to the pink rose-draped coffin.

Eliza tugged at her mother's coat sleeve and said, "Mom, Edward's crying."

Sister didn't hear her daughter. How did she not hear her own children? She didn't hear the one who was crying, and she didn't hear the one who was asking her to help him.

Did it rain? Did it snow? Was the weather freezing cold or was her broken heart simply numbed by the shock of losing this woman who had been mother to her?

A chiseled grin refuted Sister's grieving eyes.

She didn't cry, not a tear. Grandee would have been pleased she kept the promise.

At the conclusion of the service of which she didn't remember a single word, dirt was shoveled onto her grandmother's coffin. Sister stared at the workman with indignation.

An arm encircled her body and invaded her turmoil.

"Yes?" she snapped.

"Oh, I'm sorry, you must be the granddaughter," said a woman. She introduced herself saying she used to work with Sarah at the auditorium. Apologizing again, she offered her condolences.

"Thank you for being here." Sister forced a smile.

Another person, a man this time, came up; next a cousin, and then a former neighbor. Sister was surprised by the turnout for her grandmother's funeral. More than a few of the mourners asked her about Imogene.

"I'm sure Momma would have come had she been in better health," she began.

"Poor Momma, she was just so upset. We all thought it best she stay in Birmingham," she said to the next person who inquired.

One cousin mentioned privately to Sister, "I offered to pick your mother up at the airport and even invited her stay with us. Can you believe she didn't bother to say 'yea or nay?' Imogene told me that she had to *think* about it."

Sister said, "That's Momma all right."

By the fourth or fifth question regarding her mother's presence or lack thereof, Sister wanted to say, "Damnit, she's drunk like she is every day of her life!"

What she did say was, "Jack, it's really so cold, we'd better get the children out of this wind."

That ended the questions about Imogene.

As the days and weeks went by, Sister did cry. She cried when she picked up the phone to call Grandee and realized there would be no answer. She cried when she looked for Easter cards and needed one less than the year before. She cried when she put her hands into her grandmother's gray wool gloves, or saw her handwriting or went through Grandee's things at the retirement home or gave away her winter coat or passed the Denny's where they went for her birthday. Pancakes and scrambled eggs.

But Sister did smile whenever she saw a rainbow.

Two years after Grandee's death, Sister drove to Nashville to visit her father's first cousin, Quincy Hall, and his wife Ruby. It was a hot afternoon in late summer. Sister was trying to come to grips with inheriting the task of taking care of her mother. After fifty years of dealing with his wife, Harvey Clark had finally given up on Mo. He filed for divorce and moved himself to a new life in Florida.

Himself an only child, Quincy loved Sister. And he loved Harvey as dearly as he would have loved a brother. Quincy invited Sister to go along for an afternoon walk with his two big dogs.

Quincy began by asking Sister about her mother. "She's doing okay, I guess."

The fact was, Sister saw very little of Mo. Her mother stayed drunk. Sister and Quincy walked along with the dogs. A plane flew overhead. Quincy stated emphatically, "Your mother was the just about the most beautiful young woman I think I ever saw."

Sister nodded and shrugged her shoulders. It was hard for her to think of Mo being young, much less beautiful. She could only picture her as she had been since 1963, the year Sister graduated from high school. Her image for more than twenty years had been that of a passed-out body in a dirty house dress, one shoe on, her magazine dropped to the floor partially covering the bare foot. The ever-blaring television played on and on all day everyday as cigarettes smoldered in the overflowing ashtray.

That was the mother Sister "visited" whenever she drove to Birmingham to check on her. As she and Quincy walked along, Sister reviewed her many trips from Atlanta to Birmingham. *At least Daddy left Momma financially intact*, she thought.

Usually, Mo would be passed out on the living room sofa. First, Sister would put out her mother's burning cigarettes and empty the overflowing gold ceramic ashtray. She grew adept at being quiet as she sneaked about checking the house. Mo was like an evil sleeping giant, one who should not be awakened. Sister would write a hasty "Sorry I missed you" note and escape quickly to her car and drive home to Georgia. Duty done.

Quincy mused, "I remember the first time Harvey brought Mo to see us. She was tiny and blond and full of life."

"Really?" Sister answered. That image was confused with the stumbling wreck of a woman who served raw chicken. It had been years, but she could still feel the tension in her stomach.

"Just eat it," her father had said.

When Sister protested, he warned, "We don't want to set her off."

His plan generally backfired. Whether the chicken were eaten or not, Mo would find something that made her erupt. Sister could see herself sitting across from her parents. Mo glared first at Harvey then at Sister and then back with increasing rage at Harvey. The drama always ended the same way. Slamming down a fork, Mo would rise up from her seat, shriek loudly a string of curse words and storm out of the dining room. She would then fall up the five steps to where the bedrooms were located and stagger to her room. Mo would slam the door with such force the whole house shook.

With Mo, there was no winning. As an adult, and even as a wife, Sister forced herself, like a dumb, whipped dog, to continue to spend time with her parents. Those evenings inevitably ended with Harvey and Sister going for a drive waiting for the dust of the battle to settle and for the monster to pass out in her cave.

Quincy was intent on convincing Sister that her parents, at one time, were both very much in love with each other. He said, "Years ago, your folks came to Nashville for a few days. Apparently, your mother needed to be granted some kind of an annulment from her first marriage; I don't know the specifics since I'm not Catholic. But what they wanted was to have—"

Sister stopped dead in her tracks in the middle of the road. "First marriage?" she exclaimed, "Quincy, what on earth are you talking about? Momma never had another husband."

The color drained from Quincy's fading red hair and from every freckle on his weathered face. "You didn't know?" he stammered. "I'm so sorry. I thought...I thought..." He stopped helplessly.

She couldn't answer. His words, "first marriage" were suddenly streaked across the Tennessee sky as if by an army of skywriting airplanes.

Another skeleton had tumbled out of the Sinclair-Clark family closet.

On the drive back to Atlanta, Sister tried to unscramble her thoughts. She finally decided that as soon as she could fly to Tampa, she would question her father about Quincy's story. She needed to see his reaction, face to face. She had to watch his eyes as he responded.

After so many years of deception by omission, his reaction appeared to be one of relief. Curiously, her father merely nodded and sighed. "Yes, I wish Quincy had kept his big mouth shut, but he's right."

Somewhat reluctant to elaborate at first, he eventually added a few specifics to Quincy's sketchy information. He said, "Your mother was married for a very short time, but it was only a few weeks before the Sinclairs arranged for a quick divorce. Apparently, the family thought she had chosen badly. She was very young at the time. Beats me, I never really knew why they felt that way."

Harvey took a sip of ice water. "Mo and the guy drove across the state line to Arkansas. They eloped. I'm not sure they even had a home together." He gulped down the water. "I think that's about it."

"Interesting," said Sister. "I never dreamed that was the reason you and Momma weren't permitted to get married in the church. I always assumed you got married by a justice of the peace because you were both drunk."

Harvey laughed, "That was probably true, too."

"Great. So who was the first husband?" she pushed her father.

"Honestly, I can't remember his name," he said.

Sister mimicked his response, "Honestly." Harvey didn't catch her sarcasm.

10

In January 1987, Sister, Jack, Eliza, William, and Edward had just sat down to dinner to celebrate Edward's part in a school play. The Sanfords' phone rang. Sister's son William ran to answer it. "It's for you, Mom," he said. "Some lady says she has to talk to you about Grandma."

"Oh no, please no," said Sister as she got up from the dinner table.

The voice belonged to Mo's neighbor of twenty years, Mrs. Durden. "I'm sorry to bother you, but there's been a problem," Mrs. Durden said. "You'd better come quickly, Sister. The police won't go inside without a family member."

Sister's stomach dropped.

"Family member," that would be her. Sister was the only person it could be. To her this was the staggering reality, the one she had feared for years. She was in charge of Mo. "Daddy, where the heck are you?" she groaned aloud. She looked at Jack and cupped the telephone with her hand. "What can I do?" she pleaded.

"I guess you'll have to go," he said.

Through the window, Sister could see the snow falling outside. Her head started to hammer. "Yes, ma'am, of course I'll come. I can get there in three hours." She wanted to scream.

The snow was sticking. All the way to Birmingham, the windshield wipers moved the falling snow around on the windshield. More and more fell. "Die, just die, Momma," she said. "Please, God, don't do this to me."

What had Mrs. Durden said? "Your mother is on the floor. We can see her through the window. You'd best hurry."

Our Father, who art in heaven, please, fix this mess. *Hallowed be thy name.* I can't do it! *Thy kingdom come, thy will be done.* "God, this *isn't* your will," she begged.

Mrs. Durden had mentioned, "She's not moving much."

Give us this day our daily bread and forgive us our trespasses as we forgive? "Forgive?" she asked aloud in her car. "How can anyone possibly forgive all of the things Momma's done?"

Not moving much? A good sign, thought Sister.

Mo was drunk. Again. Sister didn't want to get there. She wanted to wreck. The snow pelted the glass. "Just let her die," prayed Sister.

She exited into Mountain Brook, down Euclid Avenue, and turned on her blinker. The familiar knot tightened in her chest as she pulled onto Mo's street. A patrol car, a fire truck, and an emergency vehicle sat in her mother's driveway. The policeman's blue light magnified her fear. She turned into the driveway. "Damnit all." She puffed out her cheeks and let the air escape through her lips.

She took a deep, bracing breath and forced herself out of her station wagon. "Thank you for coming. I'm the daughter," Sister muttered to the approaching police officer. "You must be freezing out here."

The policeman told her the nice lady next door had kept them in coffee. "We're fine," he said.

"Nice lady," Sister said, thankful for the understanding officer.

Sister only hoped the fire department could be as understanding. The Mountain Brook Fire Department made countless emergency runs to Mo's home over the twenty years she was there. Thanks to them, most of Mo's fires were confined to sofas. The firemen always managed to carry the burning furniture outside before the living room suffered significant damage. Smoke stained the walls, of course, but there seemed little reason to repaint every time. The only pieces of furniture Mo Clark purchased during the last thirty-five years of her life were four brand new sofas.

That cold night, Sister Sanford acted as if she were grateful to everyone who had gathered in her mother's front yard, especially to the Durdens. "Thank you so much for being here. I'm sure Momma will appreciate all you're trying to do," she said, patting the woman's hand. Sister made her way toward the brick steps to go inside.

The truth was that Sister was not feeling grateful to anybody. She resented the firemen, she resented the police, and she resented the neighbor for calling her. Hands trembling with emotion, she jammed her key into the front door. It swung open to reveal Mo on the floor, barefoot, wearing only a slip. Beside her, an empty bottle of vodka.

Sister and the policeman knelt beside her.

"What the hell are you all doing here?" Mo mumbled.

"Momma, you've fallen," her daughter said.

Gathering her wits, Mo slurred, "I've been a little under the weather, Sister."

Sister made a pleading call to an attorney, a close friend, to secure a court order to take her mother to a hospital. Within an hour, he appeared like an angel of mercy with the necessary paper work. Sister vaguely remembered signing something and being warmly embraced. She thought she heard, "Don't worry now. Things will be okay soon, the ambulance is on the way."

Minutes later, Mo was carried out of her house. A second police officer drove Sister's car to the hospital. She rode with her mother in the ambulance. How hideous the ambulance was. Lights flashed, the siren blared, Sister felt as if she were on a rocket streaking through the streets of Birmingham, a spectacle for gawkers.

Mo's extended stay in the hospital was just beginning.

Mo looked like a homeless person, and Sister was being treated like "the brute." Being questioned by the hospital's social worker, it was as if she were being held accountable for her mother's deplorable condition. The viciously-raving drunk woman, dehydrated and undernourished, now battling pneumonia, writhed on the examination table in a hospital blanket.

For four days her mother struggled for breath. Sister pleaded for mental healthcare, alcohol treatment, anything, all to no avail. Day four, Mo emerged from an oxygen tent.

"Hello, Momma. Are you feeling better?"

Her mother groused, "Get me a cigarette."

Sister replied, "Momma, I'm sorry. They won't let you have one."

Mo spit out her next three words, "Thanks for nothing."

Sister returned to Atlanta and to her family.

Sister always had a persistent small voice urging her to do the right thing. She resented that voice, and she tried to avoid it when it forced her back and forth from Atlanta to Birmingham for the next four weeks to visit her mother in an intermediate patient care hospital.

That was bad enough. Mo called her daughter from that hospital late one Thursday night. Sarah Imogene Sinclair Clark demanded, "Sister, this is Momma. Get me out of here. Get me out of here at once!"

The floor dropped from beneath Sister's feet. "Momma?"

"Just do it!" shouted Mo. Then she slammed down the phone.

Sister held her receiver twisting it as if to choke away her mother's words.

"What's wrong?" asked Jack.

"I've got to move Momma here."

"My God, are you sure you want to do that?" asked Jack.

"I haven't got a choice," replied Sister.

Jack was silent.

"Heaven help us," prayed Mo's daughter.

Sister called Catholic Social Services the next afternoon. The agency was able to locate a private care home with 24-hour care not too far from the Sanfords. There was a room available for Mo. Edith, the benevolent lady who ran the facility, had a beautiful rose garden and, more than that, she had an exceptionally patient attitude.

Mo settled in quickly. She went on outings to the grocery store with the lady and out to lunch with Sister. Mo read and watched television. Jack and the children sometimes went with Sister to visit on a Sunday.

"Mom, Grandma isn't as scary looking as she used to be," remarked Edward after one such occasion.

Sister walked into Mo's room one morning to take her out to eat. If it hadn't been her mother's room, she may not have recognized her. Mo's hair looked nicely styled for the first time in years.

"Momma!" she exclaimed.

"They cut the damn stuff off," she replied.

Edith said, "I took your mother to my beauty parlor. Doesn't she look lovely?"

"Indeed she does," said Sister.

"You both need your heads examined," growled Mo.

"See, she likes her new look," insisted Edith.

Later, Edith even managed to talk Mo into making her once famous cornbread dressing for the other ladies who lived in the home. She saved some to give to Sister who exclaimed, "It's delicious, Momma."

"If you say so," grumbled Mo.

Then, one day in the late spring, Mo called her daughter at home. "I'm going back to Birmingham now," she announced. She added, "Sister, you can either plan to take me or I will get myself there."

Reluctantly, happily, fearfully, joyfully, relieved, and with great apprehension, Sister gave her mother her way, once again. Jack volunteered to drive her. For her own peace of mind, Sister decided to absolve herself of that responsibility. Her husband took his mother-in-law back to her home. He stocked her kitchen with groceries, wished her success and returned to Sister and their children.

For several months, Sister traveled over to Birmingham periodically. Sometimes she even found her mother sober, but the next trip she'd find the closed eye, the dropped jaw, the burning cigarette, and the mouth. "You aren't supposed to be here today, idiot."

Sometimes Sister sent her mother cheerful greeting cards. That was the least threatening thing for herself that she could figure out to do. "It's something," Sister rationalized.

They talked on the phone, except, of course, when Mo was again "under the weather." Often she didn't want to answer the "damn thing." Eliza, William, and Edward succeeded in keeping Sister's mind focused in Atlanta.

In the fall of the following year, Sister was working late at a new job. Her phone line lit up. The voice said, "Sister Sanford? Are you the daughter of Mrs. Imogene Clark?"

"Yes."

"I'm afraid I have some bad news for you." Mo's new neighbor announced, "Your mother is in the hospital. We think she has broken her hip. Hip replacement may be the only real option if it's broken."

"Shit."

Sister immediately headed home and started to pack for what well could have turned into an extended stay in Birmingham. The very thought of it sent a shudder throughout her body. On the door of her closet she hung a navy blue dress in case she needed something dark for a memorial service. "Am I being pessimistic or optimistic?" she asked herself.

"Well, at least it's not snowing," she said as she got into her car.

Mrs. Lyles, the neighbor who had called Sister about Mo's broken hip, was a genuinely kind person.

One Christmas she had even brought Mo an artificial Christmas tree and some nicely wrapped gifts. Mo watched from her sofa in a bleary stupor as Mrs. Lyles and her children decorated the tree for her. She later commented to Sister, "It was a stupid thing for them to do, but I did like the bedroom slippers." In the letter that Sister wrote to thank the neighbor, she lied a little, *Momma was overwhelmed and delighted with your thoughtfulness. Oh yes, and she just loves the slippers.*

That Christmas morning Sister, Jack, and the children stood at Mo's front door, bracing for the encounter.

"Why do we have to do this, Dad?" Eliza complained.

"Because your mother wants us to," he explained.

"It will be all right. Poor Grandma," Sister said, as usual talking to herself as much as to her children. "You guys know we're all she has."

"What about Papaw?" asked Edward. "Why can't he come see her anymore?"

"'Cause they're divorced," said William, adjusting the packages in his arms.

Sister said, "Papaw is busy in Florida."

"I was busy with my new Christmas stuff," Edward offered, "and I came."

"That's because you're a great kid," said Sister.

"Here we go, folks," said Jack as he rang the doorbell.

Once inside Mo's house, the family discovered the holiday surprise. A sober Mo was seated in front of a seven-foot Christmas tree, her first one in years!

William had been so thrilled to see his Grandma up and sitting in front of the tree that on their return trip he became extremely enthusiastic. "Let's come back real soon, Mom," he urged. "We could come and clean up Grandma's house. Dad and I will cut the grass, rake her leaves, that sort of stuff." Actually, that was rake the leaves *out of the house*. Mo's house was so appallingly dirty there were even leaves in the living room and kitchen. William continued, "And you could get everything inside all nice and clean for her."

He waited for his mother to answer. She could only cry.

"Mom, why are you crying?"

"Because you're so sweet," she said.

Even in her mounting state of panic about what might be lying in wait for her, Sister could recall that day and it gave her joy. But still, Sister was angry. She was angry at her father. She was angry at Mo. She was angry at the neighbor, Christmas tree not withstanding. After all, wasn't it Mrs. Lyles who called and shamed her back into Mo's problems. Mostly, she was angry at herself. Sister was simply too disjointed even to pray.

"Why did I let her talk me into letting her live alone in that house again?" she said out loud to no one.

"Poor Momma. You must be terrified," she babbled as if Mo were there. "You hate hospitals. You hate doctors even more. Poor hospital, poor nurses, poor doctors."

Sister finally arrived at the hospital. Different hospital, same sensation. She pulled into the parking deck and stopped. Sister could feel the blood throbbing in her fingertips, through her eyeballs. Her stomach rumbled. Up the elevator she rode. The doors opened to a nurses' station.

"Mrs. Clark is in the room two doors down on your right," said the nurse.

"Well, here I go." She walked into the room. Mo lay in bed, looking thin and pale, uncomfortable and agitated. She wore the standard blue print hospital gown, her hair was twisted up into a knot that made her face appear all the more severe. An IV tethered Mo to the wall behind her as her broken eyeglasses balanced tentatively on the bridge of her nose. Untouched broth cooled on her tray.

"Hi, Momma. Are you in much pain?"

"Damn mess," she muttered.

"Can I do anything for you?" asked Sister helplessly.

"You can go back where you belong," replied her mother. "I don't know why the fools called you in the first place."

"Because they knew I'd want to be here with you," said Sister. Both women had to know she was lying.

Eventually, the anesthesiologist came in and began putting Mo under in preparation for surgery. Soon afterwards, she was wheeled down the hall and onto the elevator. Her daughter followed dutifully.

Sister sat in the waiting room surrounded by other people's families. She was as alone as if she were stranded on the moon. It was her choice, hers and Mo's. Mo had no friends, and Sister wasn't willing to share any of hers.

The doctor came out of surgery. "We've replaced your mother's hip with a new prosthesis. She's doing just fine. After a few weeks of physical therapy, I can assure you she'll be as good as new," he exclaimed cheerily.

"Thank you, doctor," she said as she forced a smile.

After an extended period of physical rehabilitation at a hospital in Birmingham, a medical ambulance brought Mo to Atlanta for a six-week stay in a nursing home located ten minutes away from the Sanfords' house. Unfortunately for her caregivers, Mo's intolerance was left undamaged by the accident. One day, she simply folded her arms and refused to do one thing asked of her. Mo's physician, nurses, and physical therapists were perplexed by their patient's unyielding, obstinate streak.

The next morning, Sister was visiting when Mo refused to comply with the staff. "Momma, you've got to cooperate."

"*Hummmph*," she answered, glaring at her daughter.

With that, the determined therapist attempted to coax the patient out of her stubborn refusal by joking.

Mo wasn't about to fall for the woman's tactic. Her brow furrowed, her eyes flared. Mo gritted her teeth and pointed angrily at Sister. She snarled and announced, "Being bull-headed runs in the family."

Sister looked at Mo and burst out laughing. "You're right, Momma," she said boldly. "We are both extremely bull-headed!" The physical therapist and a passing nurse's aide started to giggle. Remarkably, so did Mo.

It was a beginning.

As Mo's attitude started to improve, so did her body. Less than the scheduled six weeks had passed, and Sister was able to move her mother from the nursing home to Marion Manor, a Catholic personal care home. Once there, she progressed even faster. Soon the two of them could go out for a quick meal. Often it would be for breakfast. Mo liked bacon and eggs. Sometimes they went for barbeque, sometimes it was for a hamburger.

During one of their earlier adventures away from Marion Manor, Sister attempted to put into practice an exercise suggested by a well-meaning Christian friend, "to look for the face of Christ in your mother's." So once they were seated at their table, Sister decided to try. She made herself comfortable and looked across the table at Mo. "Envision Jesus," she coached herself. "Envision Jesus."

The waitress arrived. "What do you ladies want to drink today?" she chirped.

Mo frowned, "How the hell do I know what I want to drink when I haven't decided what I'm going to eat? Hold your damn horses so I can think."

Her eyes wide, the waitress disappeared in a flash.

So did the face of the Lord.

One sunny Sunday afternoon, two courageous friends of Sister took themselves to Mo's personal care home. They went inside, asked to see Mrs. Clark and came face to face with Sister's mother.

"Hello, Mrs. Clark," Pam and Jackie ventured in unison.

"Nice to see you," Mo replied pleasantly.

Sister arrived a few minutes later. She thought she saw Jackie's car in the parking lot, but quickly dismissed the idea as she went up the stairs to Mo's room. She heard voices. The voices were laughing.

Sister checked the room number before knocking. It was Mo's room alright.

"Momma?"

"Hello to you," she said. "Your charming friends have dropped by."

The friends exchanged greetings and hugs. "I can't believe you're here. Thank you for coming," Sister said slowly.

Sister observed as her mother and the visitors continued to exchange comments about the weather and how much the city had changed since the 60s. Pam, who had lived in Atlanta since she was fourteen years old, humored Mo when she agreed with her assessment about there being too much progress.

"Yes, ma'am, you're right. Nothing is like it used to be."

Concluding the visit, the group bid good-bye to one another. Her friends' mission was complete. As Sister walked Pam and Jackie out, Pam commented, "Well, Sister, I've just got to say, it's a mystery to me. I don't know how something as tiny as your mother can cause so much trouble!"

Sister shook her head in disbelief as her friends drove off.

Eliza, now a sophomore at St. Pius X High School spent several hours each month at the home where her grandmother was recuperating. Puzzled by her daughter's dedication, Sister said, "Sweetheart, of course, I'm happy you see Grandma so frequently, but please don't feel like you have to go as often you do."

"Mom, I like to go," replied Eliza.

"You do?"

"Mom, I love being with Grandma," Eliza said. "She sits there in the smoking room, puffing on her Kools and grunts and grumbles about everything."

"Uh-huh," replied Sister.

Her daughter continued, "She makes fun of the 'old folks.' She imitates them. Mom, she's real funny."

"Funny?"

Late that fall Jack's parents, Mary and Ed, came to Atlanta to watch William play football at Marist School. The next day, Mary, who had listened to Sister's struggles with Mo for years, offered to go by and visit Mo. She hadn't seen her in years.

Sister was shocked, "Are you sure you want to do this?" she asked.

"Why not? Let's go," Mary insisted.

They went. Mo was cordial, but it was obvious, she was not pleased that Jack's mother had seen her in an "old folks home." In fact, Mo was at the point where she referred to the place as the "lunatic asylum." As they left, Mo thanked Mary. "I appreciate your effort," she said. She frowned at Sister.

When they got outside, Mary said she felt nauseous. They stopped at a convenience store for something cold to drink. As she sipped her drink, Sister's mother-in-law began to rally.

"I'm so sorry to say this," Mary commented, "but I believe your mother is one of the saddest people I've ever known."

Sister set her own drink down. "I beg your pardon?"

Mary shook her head. "I just don't think I have ever met anyone who seems as lonely."

Sister paused. "I never thought about her in that way." She thought for a minute and said, "Mary, Momma always insisted she wanted peace and quiet." She was beginning to see her mother through the eyes of others.

Mary responded, "Sometimes folks don't know what they really want."

"Maybe not."

A few days later, Mo called Sister. "I'm gonna get the hell out of this place."

There was the mother she knew. "Hang on, Momma, it may take a while for me to find you a place."

"We don't have a while," she barked back.

"I'll see what's available, an apartment maybe?" Sister responded cheerfully.

"I don't care," Mo grumbled. "I may just go back to Birmingham."

"Please, Momma, give me a just few days to find something," Sister pleaded. She knew full well her mother wasn't good at being patient; more significantly, she also knew she wasn't nearly capable of taking care of herself.

Sister hung up the phone and ate an entire bag of sour cream and chive potato chips as she contacted first one retirement complex and then another. By the end of the week, she found two possibilities. They would see the first one on Monday.

A lovely senior high rise had an apartment available: a one-bedroom with a large living room, dining room, a nice bath and ample storage. Just off the kitchen there was a porch where Mo could grow her flowers. The place seemed absolutely wonderful for her mother.

Amazed with her own accomplishment in finding such an ideal solution, Sister enthusiastically picked up her mother and drove her over to see it. A lady took them on a quick tour of the apartment before they adjourned to her office.

"It's only a formality, of course," said the lady, "but we do have a few questions for you, Mrs. Clark, and there will be some forms for you to fill out."

"No big deal, Momma," assured Sister.

"And, oh yes, Mrs. Clark," she added, " you will have an entrance interview."

Mo was not eager to chat. Sister excused herself to the lobby. Still being optimistic, Sister sat and waited for her mother to return, expecting to see a big smile on her face. Before Sister could read two paragraphs of a magazine article, Mo charged out of the office. "Let's go," she commanded.

"What happened?" appealed Sister.

"The fool asked me if I'd graduated from high school!" Mo said outraged. "The nerve! Couldn't the moron tell I had sense?"

That evening, Sister explained the disaster to Jack. "Momma blew her interview. I couldn't believe it."

Jack tried to soothe his wife. He teased, "So Mo was turned down by the country club, was she?"

"Very funny."

Fortunately, the next day went better. Mo Clark went for the second possibility. There wouldn't be an interview. Of course, she would pay twice as much rent for half as much living space, but at least she didn't have to answer any more "ridiculous" questions. Mo was appeased so Sister could breath a sigh of relief.

Mo was set to move into her new place in three weeks.

The big day finally arrived. Jack and Sister picked Mo up at the personal care home. She was packed and waiting in the living room. "I am ready to go," she announced.

The nun in charge smiled broadly, "Yes, indeed she is."

The Sanfords loaded all of Mo's clothes and other items she'd accumulated into their station wagon. Sister thanked the kind nun for all she had done. Jack and Sister then drove Mo Clark over to East Paces Road to her new place. They walked Mo into her apartment for the very first time.

She made a beeline for a familiar chair, one from her home on Heritage Circle. Mo looked around the living room. She casually inspected the kitchen nook and then her new bedroom.

Mo proclaimed, "This will do all right, Sister. You two can go home now."

They did, gladly, but Sister had to hide the foolish grin she felt rising inside. It appeared she had actually made her mother happy.

11

As pleased as she appeared to be on first seeing her apartment, it still took Mo a few months to adjust to her new home. Her largest adjustment was to her apartment's smoke alarm. It was located in the kitchen, just above her stove. The second time she set it off, she was attempting to fry bacon.

The security guard, the lady at the desk, and three concerned tenants rushed to Mo's apartment. Inside they could hear the insistent beeping of the alarm. Apparently, none of the worried band of responders had as much experience with firefighting as did Mo. She had simply opened the window and was busily fanning the smoke with her *True Detective* magazine when they all started frantically pounding. "Mrs. Clark, are you all right, dear?" they cried.

It irritated her to have to stop fanning.

"Yes, what is it?" she asked hastily, jerking the door open, the magazine still in her hand. She had already tossed the skillet and its contents, her eagerly anticipated breakfast, into the kitchen sink.

"We heard your alarm," they said in a chorus.

She assured the group, "Well, as you can see, everything is perfectly fine."

One of the neighbors leaned into her living room. Mo stepped toward the woman to block her view. Smiling broadly, Mo remarked, "I do thank you all so much. Good-bye now." As she closed the door, Mo scowled, "Idiots, for God's sake, it was just some smoke."

Later she told Sister that one of the "nosy women" nearly fell over a chair as she craned her neck trying to check out what she had inside. "The damn fools were banging on my door. I've never seen such commotion over a little bit of smoke," Mo complained.

From that morning on, with the one exception of boiling water for her instant coffee, Sister's mother not only refused to cook on the top of her stove, but she also kept her kitchen window opened at all times. That window remained wide open regardless of the weather or whether a burglar might have been canvassing the rooftop. None of that mattered to her. Mo Clark's window was not going to be closed again. And whenever Mo wanted breakfast, she would call Sister and mother and daughter would go out.

In the nine years she lived in her apartment, Mo held on to her independence fiercely. "Momma, are you sure you don't want me to pick up some things for you at the grocery store?" Sister would ask. "I'm going for us anyway."

"No, thanks," she replied, "You wouldn't get the right brands. Besides, I'm going in the van with the rest of the inmates."

And, for the first time in years, Mo was getting her hair done regularly. She went each week to the beauty shop. Located downstairs in her building, the shop not only was a place of hair washing, curls, and permanents, but it was also a haven for conversation. Mo, of course, simply took plenty of reading material with her. "I'm not much for the silly chit chat," she explained. She did listen in.

Once, maybe twice, she participated in activities planned for the residents by the social director. Mo said, "I couldn't care less about the birthday parties and worse, the horrible sing-a-longs. Gawd." She grimaced. "And you could forget the group discussions on current events. Nobody can hear anything anybody else says! It's a waste of my precious time. I'd rather watch television."

"I heard you loud and clear, Momma."

Just when Sister had given up on her mother's social life, Mo told her that she had agreed to join the other residents for a trip out to the State Farmers' Market.

"Good for you, Momma. I hope it will be fun for you."

Unfortunately, it wasn't what Mo had expected. When Sister went by to see her later that week, she inquired with hopeful enthusiasm, "Well, how was the Farmers' Market?"

"Don't ask," she said. "But honestly, you should have seen those old ladies dawdling around carrying on so about squash! There weren't any fall flowers to speak of," she fussed. "I thought we'd never get back here. From now on, I'll keep my trips limited to the grocery store."

Sister never brought up the subject again.

One of Mo's boycotts was actually productive. She refused to use the building's cafeteria for almost a year until it replaced individual sugar packets, the ones that have to be torn open.

"I hate those damn packets," she fumed. "Getting them open is worse than cracking eggs." Mo held out, and eventually, the cafeteria's management gave in.

"I'm proud of you, Momma," praised Sister.

A second concession she refused to make was that of going for checkups to a physician. She never went. Not once. The dentist was to remain the only doctor with whom she would make an appointment. Mo worried about her teeth. She often remarked, "The rest of me can take care of itself."

She insisted, "I don't enjoy poor health. I'm a confirmed Christian Scientist." And that was that.

Eliza was right. Grandma was funny.

From time to time, Mo would reluctantly agree to go over to Sister's house. Of course, she had to qualify her visit by saying, "I put up with you and the children because I enjoy your dog." Nestle, an eighty-five-pound, brindle, mix German Shepherd-Golden Retriever, got along with every person on earth except the UPS driver.

Slowly, though, Mo grew closer to Sister and her family. Trust also began to grow, though painstakingly. Never one who had a mind for business dealings, Mo allowed Jack to manage her certificate of deposit that provided her some monthly income. Mo was keenly aware that her monthly dividend was a specific amount. When rates changed, the amount of her CD's dividend dropped considerably. In fact, Mo's check that month was some $200 less than it had been the month before.

On Monday, she called Sister. "Is Jack still taking care of the money thing?"

"Momma, I'm sure he is. I'll check with him."

Tuesday, Mo again called. "About the money thing, has there been any change?"

"Yes, Jack said that the interest rate on your CD has dropped a bit, Momma. Do you want me to have him call you?"

Mo said, "Forget it." She hung up the telephone. Sister heard it in her mother's voice. There was no doubt. She had been drinking.

Wednesday. Her words were slurred. "What are you two doing with my damn money?" she ranted.

"Not a thing, Momma. What are you saying?"

Sister's question was answered with a violent slam of the receiver.

Thursday. Jack came home from work, Sister had just answered the phone. "It's Momma again," she mouthed with her lips. She rubbed her temple wearily.

Jack said, "Here, give it to me."

"Mo, what's the problem?" Jack asked as he took the receiver. Finally he said firmly, "Listen to me, Mo. I have explained it all to you before. Your interest rates are going to vary. That's just the way this kind of investment works. It will soon go back up. I assure you, Mo."

She made a comment.

He responded.

She countered.

"No!" he yelled. "Your daughter is not stealing your money, nor am I!" Then, in a tone, Sister had rarely heard her husband use, he said, "Don't make such a ridiculous accusation. And, while I'm at it, Mo, don't you ever call over here when you're drinking."

She never did again. From that day on, it seemed that Mo began to trust not only her daughter, but she also trusted her son-in-law as well.

Mo's trust in her son-in-law was evident a few weeks later when the pair were in Jack's car together. Mo suddenly said, "I suppose I should have gone to Mother's funeral."

Jack shifted momentarily in his seat. He replied, "Mo, you know you couldn't have been there. You weren't feeling well enough to fly to Memphis."

"Hmm," replied Mo. She looked out the window. "Maybe you're right. My back was acting up."

Jack swallowed a moment of sarcasm. "How is that bad back of yours doing in the car today?"

"Ask me no questions, I'll tell you no lies," she responded.

"Why don't we stop for a sandwich, Mo? Maybe some barbeque will get your mind off things," he suggested. "I'm hungry, you must be, too."

"If you insist," she said.

A few miles later, Jack and Mo were being served barbeque.

As Mo lifted her sandwich, she paused. "I don't know why Sister is doing so much for me. I don't deserve it."

Jack put down his fork, looked at her and said, "Mo, there's always time to prove you do deserve it."

Sister could only gape when Jack told her the story.

The years passed quickly. The Sanford children grew up. Eliza and William were in college, Edward was in high school. Mo mellowed as she moved into her late seventies and eighties. Jack continued to handle Mo far better than most people were able to do. And Sister continued to heal.

Holidays became times divided equitably with the grandparents. A time or two Jack's parents came to Atlanta and Mo joined everyone for dinner.

Each Christmas after they ate, Mo, Jack, Eliza, William, Edward, and Sister would gather in the den. Mo would marvel at the boxes stacked by her chair. "You shouldn't have done so much," she said as she opened each of the children's gifts, those from Sister and Jack and even from the Sanford's pets. One Christmas there was a tin of cookies, a sterling silver puppy-dog pin, and a carton of cigarettes, to which she said, "Well, Sister, I suppose at long last you're going to stop complaining about my cigarettes?"

"No, Momma, I'm just saving you the trip to the store."

As Mo unwrapped the rest of her presents, she found some blue pajamas along with a Whitman's Sampler, and a book with pictures of gardens located throughout the world. She commented, "I'll enjoy this book. My goodness, I have so many nice pretties!"

She methodically folded and stacked all the wrapping paper and saved each bow and to-from tag.

"You've all gone to too much trouble," she insisted.

She then turned the attention to her gifts for the Sanford family. She did her "shopping" in a charmingly singular way. Each year, she gave Jack and Sister $26.50 in cash. That was $25, *plus tax*. In separate envelopes, she enclosed for each grandchild exactly $10.60 or $10 plus tax. Not to overlook anyone, she provided for her favorite Nestle and both the Sanford cats. The inclusion of the cats was another big concession for her, because she openly and ardently detested felines. Nonetheless, Mo treated the pets equally: $1.06, $1 plus tax, to be spent exclusively on pet treats.

Between Christmas and New Years, the Sanfords received a detailed thank you note in which Mo indexed every item she had received, by whom it was given and descriptions of how each package was wrapped.

"*TaTa, Love, Momma, Grandma, Mo*"

Years after Eliza had outgrown any interest she had in playing with Mo's dollhouse, Sister decided to decorate it for the upcoming Christmas season. Just as she had as a child, Sister enjoyed setting it up, placing the furniture, the little family, the holiday decorations. When Mo inspected the result of

Sister's efforts, she responded "Why do you always go to so damn much trouble?"

The next year Sister didn't bother to do it again, and Mo asked why she hadn't. From that Christmas on, the dollhouse was decorated.

One Christmas, Mo and Sister stood admiring the dollhouse. Sister had purchased many new miniature accessories that season and had filled the four rooms with all manners of festive decor. Greenery and ribbon outlined the stairway, doors, and windows; with bows on the furniture and a bowl of holly on the antique sewing machine which was a copy of Grandee's. Sister had two nativity scenes; one under the downstairs Christmas tree and a second on the hallway table. There were button-sized gifts for members of the dollhouse family. Santa and his reindeer stood poised atop the roof.

"I added a second tree, see over in the corner of the bedroom?" said Sister, pointing to the new addition.

"Nice touch," agreed Mo.

"And look at the miniature tea set. See the Christmas design on the cups?" Sister said as she pointed to the coffee table in front of the sofa. "Can you believe there can be so much detail on something that tiny?"

The phone rang. "Hello," Sister answered. "Could I call you back later on this afternoon? Momma and I are busy. We're playing with Eliza's dollhouse." She laughed as she said goodbye to her friend.

Mo made a face at her daughter and said, "Whoever that was probably thinks we're a couple of nuts."

"Momma, we are."

"I suppose you're right," Mo replied. She didn't want her daughter to notice, but she smiled.

Sister did see the smile.

"And what's that?" Mo asked, gesturing to an object in the corner of the kitchen. "Does that say 'Reindeer Food?'" she asked.

"Yes, isn't that cute?" responded Sister.

"I think there's as much clutter in here as you have in your home," grumbled Mo. "Dust catchers, I call it."

"I like clutter."

"Suit yourself," said Mo.

"Oh, and look at these little bitty books. They fit perfectly into the bookcase by the window. I put one in the mother's arms so it looks as if she's reading to her daughter.

Mo's eyes met Sister's.

"I saved the best for last," said Sister. "Are you ready?"

"Do I have a choice?" Mo asked.

"No!" Sister said as she flipped a switch. Lights came on throughout the house.

"Oh my!" exclaimed Mo. "Will you look at that!"

Sister loved her mother's reaction. "A little light makes a big difference, doesn't it, Momma?"

"Yes, it really does!" she said. The lights reflected back into her face. Mo's eyes twinkled.

"Momma, I was afraid you wouldn't approve of all these changes."

"Oh, I'm not *that* bad," said Mo.

"No, Momma," Sister said, "you're not that bad at all."

Not only were holidays important to Mo, but she was also committed to participating in other significant family affairs. She managed to attend all three of her grandchildren's high school graduations. Two were held at the Atlanta Symphony Hall, a lovely place, indoors, air-conditioned, comfortable.

The most outstanding achievement regarding the three graduations for Grandma, however, was her final one. The youngest of the Sanfords, Edward, graduated from high school in 1995. His ceremony was held on the hottest June day in memory in his high school's brand new football stadium.

Mo, whose emphysema was worsening by the day, joined Jack's equally valiant parents, along with Aunt Maryetta and Uncle Dan, his cousin Mary Shea, the four Sanfords and a hearty contingent of friends for the afternoon-long ceremony.

Somehow, Mo made the climb to the top row in that stadium to cheer on her grandson, the graduate. Jack took her home afterwards and barely got her to her bedroom. He later remarked, "I will never know how that woman made it." Edward's thank you note for his grandmother's remarkable effort remained one of her treasured mementos. Rightfully so. Grandma had earned it.

For Mo's birthday, she went over to Sister's house to have dinner. Mo didn't celebrate her birthdays. Instead, she did agree to have an "unbirthday dinner."

Eliza and William were both in Europe for the summer, and Edward was in school in Athens with a major test scheduled for the next day. Therefore, the gathering was a small one including only Mo, Sister, Jack, and Nestle the dog.

Jack picked his mother-in-law up on his way home from work. As they came up the driveway, it was obvious to Sister that the "birthday girl" riding in the front seat of the car was frowning. "At least it's a sober scowl," she thought as she opened the back door to greet her as agreed. "Happy Unbirthday, Momma!"

"Talk about something pleasant, the weather maybe," replied Mo.

"Okay," said Sister. "Doesn't seem as hot tonight."

"It's supposed to rain," answered Mo. "I hope we don't lose the damn lights."

Mo took a seat in the den and watched the news with Jack. As she put the final touches on dinner, Sister thought back to parties of thrown dishes, ruined dinners, and embarrassment. She peeked out the kitchen. Mo was sitting peacefully watching the news.

Jack readied the grill for his part of the cooking, a filet for his mother-in-law. Mo came into the kitchen to chat as Sister warmed the rolls. She petted the dog. "You're getting old, too, Nessie," she said.

Soon they were seated around the table as the grill cooled outside. Jack and Sister talked idly through the meal, but Mo remained quiet. Even Jack's flawlessly prepared filet did not provoke comment from Mo. Sister merely assumed her mother didn't approve of something she had done. *Ah ha*, she thought. *It's the added vegetable. I shouldn't have fixed the broccoli*, she said to herself. *I knew better. Momma wants her steak with potatoes and salad only. It is her birthday, after all.*

Mo was pushing her salad around on the plate. She hadn't touched a bite.

"Oh, Momma, I'm sorry, I meant to have your thousand-island dressing."

"It's fine," said Mo. "I'm just not hungry."

"Oh dear," Sister added, "I forgot the lemon for your iced tea." She got up to get the lemon. "Your daughter is turning into a ding bat."

"Must be the hot weather," said Mo offhandedly.

As it turned out, it wasn't the broccoli, or Mo's appetite, or the weather. Three weeks later in early August, Mo finally admitted to having a sore throat. When Sister suggested a visit to a doctor, her mother came back with her traditional, "We'll see." What she meant was, "Forget that."

Sister did talk her into checking with the nurse in her building. When she called to see what the nurse thought about the sore throat, Mo said, "She can't do a damn thing. She's not competent, I guess you'd better call your doctor." Mo was furious. She wasn't accustomed to having to deal with those sorts of issues.

A few days later, Sister took her mother to the Sanford's family physician. Based on all her past experience with doctors and their lengthy forms, Sister was duly concerned when a questionnaire was immediately handed to them in her family physician's office. Sitting herself beside Mo, she said, "Relax, Momma, I'll fill this out for you. I'll just ask you some questions and fill in exactly what you want me to say. How's that?"

Mo said, "I guess so, let's get it over with."

She started to ask "age." She wisely decided against that question, even though at the time she wasn't sure whether Mo was eighty-three, eighty-four, or eighty-five.

"Let's see, Momma, address, I got that, and symptoms?"

Mo said, "A sore throat, I told them that on the phone."

Sister wrote, "persistent sore throat."

She laughed and asked, "Let's see, Momma, when was your last period?"

Mo got up to leave.

"Please sit down, Momma," Sister said calmly, resting a hand on Mo's arm. She quickly and quietly completed the forms.

The nurse called, "Mrs. Clark."

Sister picked up a magazine and settled in for the wait.

Forty-five minutes later, Mo shot out from the back of Dr. Bush's office faster than if she'd been fired from a cannon.

Sister hurried after her. "Momma, what's wrong?"

"I'm not happy with your doctor," she announced as she charged down the hall of the medical building.

They walked across the parking lot to Sister's car. Mo was moving so fast that Sister actually had to rush to keep up with her. Mo's daughter opened the car door and helped her mother in.

"What did she say about your throat?" asked Sister as they drove away.

"She's incompetent," said Mo tossing a prescription on the floorboard. "Your doctor told me *her* name used to be Imogene, but she changed it to something else. Not shortened to 'Genie' or even to 'Ima.' She changed it to something entirely different. Why in the hell would she want to tell me that?"

"Beats me," said Sister, deciding not to bring up Imogene's own pretty radical change in name to Mo. She'd best save that for a day her mother recovered from her sore throat.

At the traffic light, Sister leaned down and retrieved the prescription. "Let's at least get this filled. It might help. What is this anyway?"

Mo sat and looked out the car window.

When Sister picked up the medicine, she asked the pharmacist what he thought might be the matter with her mother based on the prescription. He said he really couldn't say for sure. Sister read the words on the bottle of capsules. It was for a "bacterial infection," so she figured the medicine would take care of whatever was wrong. She hoped so at any rate.

"So, Momma, how's your throat this morning?" Sister began some weeks later.

Mo replied, "Let's discuss something more pleasant." She coughed and reached for a throat lozenge.

"Momma, you're getting a little thin," observed Sister on another occasion.

"I hadn't noticed. Don't you have something interesting to talk about?" she snapped.

"What sounds good to eat?" attempted Sister. "How about I go and get us some hot soup for lunch?"

"I still don't have much of an appetite."

"Momma, I think we should try to see the doctor again."

"*No!*" shouted her mother. Then she began to cough. Mo choked, "Now see what you've done!"

Sister drove home and called her friend Pam. "I am beginning to think something is seriously wrong with Momma's throat."

Pam, as she always did, offered to pray.

A few weeks later, Sister called the doctor again and asked to speak with the nurse. Sister explained that Mrs. Clark was losing weight, and she believed something was seriously wrong. The nurse called back within minutes and gave her the name and phone number of a surgeon. Sister thumbed through her telephone book. The physician was a throat surgeon. Her stomach convulsed.

Sister picked her mother up for the morning appointment. As they drove down Peachtree Street, Sister pointed out Lenox Square for the umpteenth time. Sister and her mother had shopped there many times during Mo's years of sobriety during Sister's high school days. She always complained that the mall hadn't stayed the same as it was in 1959. "They ruin everything here," she fussed.

They passed Brookhaven where Sister took her each year to admire the spring flowers. "See, Momma, there's the lovely neighborhood where you like to see all the azaleas and daffodils and dogwoods."

Mo looked absently. Nothing seemed to register.

A voice in Sister coached her further to remind her mother about gentle things, special moments they had shared, about car rides and nice lunches. "Remember, Momma," she pointed out a restaurant. "Remember when we ate there?"

"I guess so," Mo commented.

"I have an idea," ventured Sister. "Do you want to go for some barbeque after we're done? We're not far from that spot you like for us to pick up sandwiches for you. Now, it's not very fancy, but here's your golden opportunity to see it in person," she asked, wishing it were possible.

"We'll see," Mo said.

Sister knew Mo didn't feel anymore like eating a sandwich than she did. There was a tempest in her own stomach. She could not imagine how her mother was feeling. Sister didn't ask as she turned the car onto Peachtree Dunwoody Road.

"It's a gorgeous day," she warbled ridiculously. "After we see the doctor, we'll shop for your groceries. You won't be disappointed about not getting to ride in the van with the ladies, I hope."

"We'll see," she said again.

Mo's ill mood increased when the medical building came into sight.

The physician didn't make them wait too long.

Sister had called the doctor's office to have the forms sent to her home. She had learned that lesson very well and filled everything out in advance of the appointment. The two of them sat in the office while Sister babbled nervously about insignificant things.

The receptionist called, "Mrs. Clark." Her mother made no protest when Sister stood up and joined her. Mo and Sister walked together into the examination room. Sister steadied her mother and was shocked to feel Mo trembling.

The physician looked into Mo's throat. He reacted and, to Sister, appeared to be quite stunned at what he was seeing, "Mrs. Clark, this does not look good. I need to discuss something of a very serious nature with both of you."

His explanation whirled into a buzzsaw of complicated medical terms that Mo had a difficult time hearing, and Sister didn't want to understand. What they heard and understood clearly was the word "cancer."

The compassionate doctor swallowed hard. He put his hand on the armrest of Mo's chair. "I am so very sorry to say this, but, Mrs. Clark, you have approximately six months to live."

Mo responded, "Call Dr. Kevorkian."

The remainder of their appointment with the throat surgeon was a blur of words and feelings, options they didn't have, pictures of what to expect and an overwhelming sense of powerlessness and terror.

There'd be no operation. "Mrs. Clark, given your age and the stage of your illness, you'd not be able to survive surgery."

No, radiation was not an option. "I'm afraid it would be too painful, much too hard on you. But, that's not the most important issue here. At this point, Mrs. Clark, I don't think radiation would buy you any time."

No, chemotherapy wouldn't help either. "Chemotherapy? I think it would be in your best interest to try to enjoy the time you have left," said the physician as he wrote out a prescription for pain killers. "Yes, you are going to die. I am so terribly sorry," he said as if he truly wished he were wrong.

12

As Sister drove Mo back to her apartment, she grasped for words to encourage her mother. Anything. Nothing came. Mo sat in the seat next to her, dazed. Finally, she said, "Humph, another incompetent doctor. What kind of doctor meets you, and five minutes later, tells you you're going to croak?"

Sister wanted to laugh.

Being angry was Mo's way to cope. It was more comfortable for her to attack the doctor than to think about the diagnosis.

They stopped for the pain medicine. Mo said, "Pick up a carton of cigarettes while you're in there."

Sister bought three cartons for her. The purchase gave the daughter the illusion of normalcy. It gave them both time.

When they arrived back at Mo's building, Sister helped Mo out of the car. They walked inside, Sister steadying her mother each step she took. The lobby was buzzing with the other residents who were gathering to take the van to the grocery store. Several people extended greetings and offered concerns about Mo's weakened appearance.

"Can I get you something at the store, dear?" asked one lady.

"I heard you weren't feeling well," said another. "Is there anything I can do to help?" she asked.

Mo didn't reply.

Sister said, "Thank you, but right now Momma is worn out and needs to rest." She nodded warmly to other familiar faces and escorted Mo into the elevator. Once inside the apartment, Sister expressed the only thing she thought might give comfort to her dying mother. Putting her arm around her frail body, Sister said, "Momma, do you understand?" She swallowed hard and whispered softly, "Momma, you're going to see your Daddy again."

Mo looked at Sister and smiled faintly. "You go on now. You've done enough," scolded Mo.

"Momma, can I please...?"

Her mother wouldn't let her finish. Mo's face contorted. "Go on, I said, just go."

Sister made her way slowly down the hall. She heard Mo quickly chain-lock the door behind her. As Sister waited for the elevator, her memory leapt about sporadically. She was at Mo's bedside for the broken hip. Then back at St. Agnes when her mother had forgotten to come to pick her up. Just as quickly, she was standing by Howard's coffin and learning that her grandfather had killed himself. Then back to last Christmas standing with Mo in front of the dollhouse.

The elevator stopped, its doors opening like great jaws ready to eat. Sister got in. She saw herself looking into Howard's coffin with Annette. The body she saw wasn't Howard's. The body was her mother's. The elevator stopped in the lobby. Sister hurried to her car, unwilling to look back.

The physician had suggested that she call him sometime in the next week. As she drove home, Sister reached for her car phone. "Yes, this is Imogene Clark's daughter. I believe he wanted to talk with me regarding my mother."

The surgeon immediately came on the line. Kind and gentle, he seemed to be almost as upset as were she and Mo. The thoughtful man began with, "I can see how close you and your mother are."

Sister clung to the words.

The doctor continued, "Mrs. Sanford, I must tell you, in all candor, that giving your mother six months to live was a very optimistic speculation."

Sister's heart plunged. She was stunned, her own healthy throat twisted in a spasm. Her eyes filled with tears and she began to cry.

She hung up. Later she couldn't remember whether or not she had said another word to the caring man.

In mid-November, Sister offered, "Momma, why don't you move in with us?"

"No, I'd never want to do that," Mo responded. "The activity at your house would drive me nuts. Don't come here if that's *all* you want to talk about," complained Mo.

Sister tried again. She was disappointed that her mother was being so obstinate. At the same time, she was encouraged that her mother was still acting like Mo.

"Hire someone?" Mo glared at her daughter. "You know I don't like to have people under foot!"

"A nurse? Sister, for God's sakes!"

Sister hung her head.

Mo wouldn't even permit a cleaning woman to come to dust and vacuum her apartment once a month. Talking to her mother, or trying to talk her mother, was like persuading an oak tree to transplant itself.

She certainly dared not mention Jack's idea of Mo going into a hospital. So again, Sister left her mother's place frustrated that they had no plan of action. As her mother waved to her from her kitchen window, Sister was oddly comforted that things remained as they were. It was daylight and her fears were at rest.

Mo Clark dealt with terminal cancer the same way she had dealt with every problem that had come her way. She ignored it. Sister had learned the same lessons at her own mother's knee. But try as they each did to ignore Mo's terminal cancer, its reality wouldn't vanish. For the next six weeks, the two women visited. And Mo, like her mother, continued to change the subject.

"How is Edward liking the University of Georgia?" she inquired. "Has William heard about his new job yet?"

Sister planned a special Thanksgiving dinner for her mother. After all, for years the two of them had spent almost every third Thursday in November together. Each yearly celebration had been an improvement over the one before.

As Thanksgiving week began, Sister began to notice her own sore throat. She started losing her voice on Monday afternoon. Fearful that she had something she could pass on to her mother, Sister decided to go to her doctor. The last thing she wanted to do was make her mother even sicker.

The first thing the doctor suggested was that Sister's illness might actually be a blessing in disguise. She said, "Sometimes contracting pneumonia or a virus can be considered an angel of mercy for the terminally ill patient. A brief illness diminishes the time of suffering for that patient."

Sister winced at the expression "terminally ill patient."

After checking Sister's throat, the physician decided that the laryngitis might be psychosomatic. She suggested it could be Sister's body's way of responding to her own inability to help her mother. "Truly, I don't see anything to indicate a serious throat infection. It could be that you are feeling powerless to do anything about your mom's condition. Your voice is shutting down in response."

That didn't prove to be the case. By Wednesday, psychosomatic or whatever the "bug" was, it managed to put Sister to bed with chills and a fever that lasted for three more days.

Mo, who in recent years had steadfastly refused to use the telephone except in the case of an emergency, called her daughter to see how she was feeling.

"Sister? Is that you? I can hardly recognize your voice!"

"Momma? What's wrong?" she asked, assuming something had happened to her mother.

"Sister, don't be silly. I'm worried about you," Mo said sweetly. She called her daughter each and every day until Sister was well.

Sister's illness did not distract her from Mo's own adamant refusal to acknowledge her own illness or to talk about her ominous future. Worried, but finally well after three days, Sister began to look into some alternatives for her care. Following the suggestion of her doctor, she contacted Hospice. An organization of health care providers and counselors, the group cares for and comforts patients and their families once the patient has been given six months or less to live. Mo qualified.

One of the first suggestions Hospice made was for the family to make some preliminary decisions about what would be done at the time of Mo's death. That included, of course, funeral arrangements and burial location.

Supported by her son William, Sister walked into a funeral home Pam had recommended. A somberly-dressed young man greeted them and ushered them into a viewing room. Upon walking into the well-appointed parlor, Sister's eyes shot to the coffin positioned at the far end of the room. She was overwhelmed by the scent of floral arrangements. "This is real—

Momma is actually going to die," she said reaching for her son's arm.

As she filled in some of the necessary forms, Sister said irritably, "Momma's right, forms are for idiots." William just looked incredulously at his mother. She was generally less out spoken. He took her hand. Squeezing her fingers, William said, "Mom, it's going to be okay."

The man showed them into the coffin display area. It was a cold room filled with coffin after coffin after coffin. William's face flushed and Sister's neck tightened.

"This is ghoulish," remarked William.

Sister wandered about staring vacantly ahead as if she were lost in a strange land. It was difficult for her to breathe and her knees were shaking uncontrollably.

The funeral director apparently sensed their discomfort and made his rehearsed, gentle, yet appropriate, remarks. Sister didn't respond to them. She was still attempting to come to terms with the fact that her stone cold sober mother, the one with a good mind, the one who made phone calls to her throughout Thanksgiving to see how she was feeling, the one who took joy in flowers and dogs, the one with a quirky sense of humor, the mother who figured in tax with Christmas money; that mother, her mother, in a very short period of time would be positioned in one of those boxes and buried six feet under the ground.

Sister pointed to one coffin. It was made of cherry wood and had soft pink lining. There was a rose for her mother to look at. Momma loved roses. Sister breathed in as she cleared her foggy brain. "My dear Lord, a rose, what difference would it make after all? Momma won't see that rose."

Sister had shared the news of Mo's terminal illness with Betty Ann. Since their teenage days, the two had stayed close and in touch. It did not surprise Sister at all that her dear friends—Betty Ann and her husband Chad—drove seven hours from their home so Betty Ann could see Mrs. Clark one last time.

When Sister phoned her mother to say she and Betty Ann were ready to come by, her mother responded, "No, I've decided. That's not a good idea."

Truthfully, Mo thought cancer was "catching." She also wanted Betty Ann to remember her as she once was, how she was when she and Betty Ann's mother chatted in the carpool line, or when their teenage daughters had sleepovers and the two commiserated, or when the girls' first children were born just two days apart.

Seven hours in the car and Mo only permitted Betty Ann to talk with her over the telephone. That was Mo. Betty Ann wasn't phased in the least. "Hey," she said in her own accepting way, "of course, I understand how your mother feels. We tried. That's all we can do."

Betty Ann spent the weekend building Sister up. She took the two of them to see an Atlanta holiday event, the Festival of Trees. They purchased a small Christmas tree and some little wooden ornaments: angels, bears, Santas, and tiny wooden soldiers. When they returned to Sister's house, the friends sat at her kitchen table and decorated the tree for Mo.

Sister took it over the day after Betty Ann left to go back home. "Put it by the television," said Mo. Admiring it, she said, "I think Betty Ann was the least peculiar of all your high school friends." Coming from Mo Clark, that was high praise, indeed.

13

With Christmas around the corner, Jack decided that the Sanfords should surprise Mo with a brand new television set, one with a remote control.

"The picture is getting worse on your mother's set, it could go any day now," he mentioned to Sister. "Mo shouldn't have to get up and down to change the channel on that old one of hers. Besides, I really don't think we'll be able to find her another TV with an old fashioned dial anyway."

His thoughtful suggestion was made before Jack fully understood that Mo had outlived her technological aptitude. Mo still couldn't understand how to operate the newly-installed climate control device in her apartment. She was truly perturbed when the workman disrupted her routine to install it in the first place. "Why do these people always have to bother me right in the middle of my stories?" she fumed. Then, after all was said and done and the work was finished, Mo didn't understand how to adjust the thermostat.

Sister had gone over to her mother's four or five different times to demonstrate the controls to her. "Momma, look, first you open the cover," began Sister once again. "Next, switch to red for heat, yes, that's right. Okay, now switch to blue for cold air. Hooray, you've got it this time!"

The two of them celebrated with a Coke. Sister opened their bottles. "Here you go."

Mo said, "TaTa."

"Now, Momma, are you sure you understand about your heat there?"

"Yes."

The following day when Sister returned, the apartment was hot even by her own cold-natured standards.

"I can't get the damn thing to work," groaned Mo. "I wish they'd left the old one. It worked fine," she said with an aggravated sigh. Sister put colored sticky notes on the warmer and cooler buttons. It made no difference, the apartment remained either far too hot or far too cold. Frustrated and irritated, her mother said. "Forget it, I'll manage."

In mid-December, a few days after the new television had arrived, Sister phoned her mother. "How's the new TV doing?" she asked.

"Can't get that infernal machine to work," fussed Mo. "I had to leave the TV on all night so I could see my stories today."

"Oh dear."

As soon as Jack had completed his after-work run around the neighborhood, Sister confronted her husband about her mother's dilemma with the television remote.

Determinedly and without stopping to eat his dinner, Jack agreed to show Mo, one more time, how to work her remote control. Dressed in his red warm-up suit, he sighed resolutely, "Come on, let's go over there." He shook his head and muttered, "Poor old soul."

They crawled through the thick 5:30 traffic. Eventually, they reached Mo's place.

Sister spoke into the call box at the apartment door. "Momma, Jack and I are here, push the button to let us in."

As she had done for nine years, Mo said, "Okay, pushing '0.'" That, she did fine. The door buzzed and in they went. Up the elevator, down the hall and to her door, Jack was on a mission. Mo had already unlocked her door. Her voice cracked, "Come in, it's open." She was sitting in her chair by the window.

"Hi, Momma. I brought Jack with me this time," Sister kissed the top of her mother's head.

"Hello, Mo. It's good to see you," said Jack as he turned to check on the new television. "Let's see what the problem is with your set."

Handing her the remote, he said, "Okay, here we go. It's just a matter of pushing a button or two." Over and over again, Mo's son-in-law attempted to show her how the remote control worked. It became readily evident to him that her eye-hand coordination was not allowing his mother-in-law to absorb what he was trying so hard to make clear. Mo wasn't just "not listening" as in the past, she actually wasn't able to take in what was being explained to her.

"Mo," he said, "I've got a new plan. Sister and I are going to go and pick up something. We'll be back in twenty minutes or so."

"Good," she said. "Now hurry. Oh, and leave the TV on because *Wheel of Fortune* is coming on in an hour."

Sister and Jack discussed Mo's worsening condition while they worked their way through the bumper to bumper traffic.

"I realize we've got to get some help for Momma, but she's like talking to a wall."

"I know," Jack agreed. "It's just so pitiful."

Finally, they returned to Mo's apartment from their long and fairly stressful mission of finding a remote control with larger buttons. Jack began to remove every button on the remote, every one that didn't seem necessary for her viewing needs. Mo certainly didn't need *surf*, *status*, or heaven forbid, *mute*. In the last week, accidentally pressing the mute button had twice sent the ailing woman into an emotional tailspin.

Jack popped out the superfluous buttons. His back was to Mo and Sister, who were sitting across the room watching, with rapt attention, his every move. He began to program the brand new remote control.

Jack's frustration grew. He shifted back and forth in his running shoes. Shoulders taunt, his red cotton warm up suit was making him feel all the hotter. Jack groaned in discomfort and irritation. At one point he turned down the heat. "Do you ladies mind?"

"No. Go ahead, honey," said Sister.

"Why's he gotta mess with that other stupid thing?" asked Mo.

"Because he's getting so hot, Momma, that's all," replied Sister.

"I see," she said sharply.

And Jack was getting hungry, really hungry.

Mo and Sister stared hopefully at Jack's back.

"How's it going now?" his tense wife tried to encourage.

Jack made no reply.

Wheel of Fortune was about to begin. Once again, Mo anxiously picked up the clock on the table beside her chair. She checked the time.

"Any minute now, Momma," assured her daughter. "Jack will have this thing up and running."

Mo kept her eyes riveted on Jack. She looked again at her clock. She was then clutching it in her lap.

He, in turn, shifted his hips. His shoulders tightened.

"Any problem?" Sister inquired of her husband.

"Umph," he uttered.

"Hold your horses, Momma," Sister chirped in a silly fashion. "I think he's just about got it. Right, Jack?'

"Ummm hummm," he groused.

Then, in a loud and audible voice, Mo asked, "Why is your husband dressed like Santa Claus?"

Jack's body jerked in reaction to Mo's commentary not only about his red outfit but also about his ample size and shape.

Sister tried to gulp down her rapidly rising hysteria. There was no use. She gave in and laughed unrestrained until the tears started to stream down her face. The laughing felt good.

Red face to match his clothes, Sister's well-intentioned husband turned around. Jack shook his head, "I am so sorry, girls. I'm afraid that I just can't get the new clicker to program."

Mo said, "Should you have taken out those buttons?"

Silence.

Then, even Jack had to laugh. "Mo, I think you're absolutely right."

He managed to turn the set on and leave it adjusted to one channel for her. He then made a promise to his mother-in-law, "Mo, we will get the damn machine straightened out for you as soon as we possibly can. But I'll also be on the lookout for another dial TV." He patted her shoulder and said, "You'll never know how sorry I am about all this confusion."

Mo said she'd simply leave her new TV on again for the night. "I'd rather do that than do without my morning news," she told them. "Now you go on home and have your dinner, because it's getting late. I want to watch my game show."

The next morning, with Jack's agreement, Sister called out the cavalry. Her son William came over with yet a third remote control. He demonstrated it and carefully wrote out simple instructions that he thought his grandmother could follow. She practiced every step as he explained each one to her. At last, because of her grandson, it seemed that Mo was finally able to make use of her brand new remote control.

Like Thanksgiving, Christmas was going to come and go without the usual festivities that had for years involved Mo. The time was oddly busy, oddly peaceful, oddly empty. Mo told Sister what to say to her grandchildren, "Tell them that I am vain, and that I don't want them to see me looking like hell."

On Christmas Eve afternoon, Mo presented Sister with a gift—Mo's prized piece of Victorian porcelain. It had been given to her own godparents on the occasion of their wedding just after the turn of the century. The piece was a white-footed basket decorated in gold with small flowers in orange, lilac, and blue. A blond cherub dressed in blue was balanced delicately in the center of the basket and flanked with larger flowers in shades of purple, orchid, yellow and rust. Mo had wrapped her treasure in an old, white, cardigan sweater.

"Sorry it's not wrapped any better," she apologized.

Sister said, "Momma, thank you so much. You know that doesn't matter!"

"Matter's to me," she said as she coughed.

"I will treasure Auntie's wedding present, Momma."

She blew her nose and Mo replied, "I kept it on the buffet."

Mo directed Sister over to the marble top desk. "Open the drawer," she said. Her voice was growing more raspy with each breath. Mo struggled. "See the envelopes?"

"Yes, Momma."

"Get them out, see if they're all there." She coughed. Mo shook another cough drop from its box and put it in her mouth.

Sister gathered eight white envelopes. There was one for Jack and one for Sister. There was an envelope for Eliza, for William, and for Edward. And Mo had remembered the pets as well. She always remembered her "Nessie" first, and then in order she remembered "those two nasty cats."

Mo had written messages on each and every envelope. Each envelope contained the recipient's Christmas money, plus tax.

The note to Sister read, *Many thanks for everything. Merry Christmas, Love, Momma.*

14

Two weeks later in early January, Sister was sitting in a traffic jam twenty miles north of Atlanta. At a stop light, she checked for messages on her answering machine. 11:35 A.M.
"Mrs. Sanford, this is Sherry Welch. I'm the manager at Mrs. Clark's apartment," said the voice. "It is urgent that I talk with you regarding your mother's condition. Please call me back immediately."

The blood surged through Sister's whole body. She pulled into a shopping center parking lot and called her at once. The woman said, "You will have to move your mother from our facility. She has become so frail. I'm afraid that Mrs. Clark is starting to upset the other residents. I'm sorry."

"I'll be right there, Miss Welch," Sister said quietly.

Observing the congested road as far as she could see, Sister made a quick U-turn and made her way back onto the expressway. Sister tried to compose herself by saying, "You'll do fine. You have a nice thirty-minute drive to gather your thoughts." She phoned Jack from her car. He quickly agreed to meet her at Mo's building.

"One day at a time." She thought of every word in the Al-Anon literature she could remember. She wished, then, she had spent more time reading it. "You can handle anything for 24 hours," she parroted. Sister prayed every mile of the way toward town. "...*Your will be done.*"

Focused as she was on her mother, she hardly had any memory of another automobile, an 18-wheel truck, a shopping center, a forest, or a building she might have seen as she made her way. Sister finally reached the parking lot of Mo's apartment. Jack waved at her from the main entrance as she found a parking space. Seconds later with Jack beside her, she sat trembling in a chair in Sherry Welch's office. Once again, just as in the hospital in Birmingham, Mo's daughter found herself under inspection.

"Of course, I am fully aware of Mrs. Clark's situation, Miss Welch. Momma has terminal cancer," Sister began. "But you also have to understand that my mother has never been one to accept anybody's suggestions. Certainly not any suggestions about her health, and most definitely, not suggestions from me. The only person who has ever made any headway with her has been my husband Jack."

The three of them talked for a few more minutes as a more composed Sister attempted to explain the options that Mo had adamantly rejected throughout her brief illness: nurses, Meals on Wheels, moving into the Sanford's home, Hospice care, hospitalization, and cleaning service.

Sister said, "Of course, I am responsible for my mother. I have been responsible for Momma for ten years," she said, feeling every prick of the resentment she thought she had long since released. She shrugged her shoulders and held out her hands, palms up. "It's unmistakable, I've become my mother's mother."

As she listened to Sister and Jack, Sherry Welch's demeanor began to soften. She looked at the distraught couple and said, "Perhaps she would listen to me. What do you two think?"

Jack shrugged. "Give it a shot," he replied.

"Miss Welch, please see what you can do," Sister said. "I'm out of ideas," she adding thanking her. Even so, neither Sister nor Jack held much hope for the woman's success. Mo's situation had no answer as far as either of them could see. Given that all of their ideas had run out several weeks into the crisis, they were more than grateful to accept her offer.

"The first thing I want you both to do is to call me Sherry," she said as she left Sister and Jack and walked to the elevator. She pushed the button for Mo's floor and called back to the Sanfords, "Please, try to relax for a minute. I'll be right back."

Sister held her breath. God, it seemed, had sent her another reinforcement. She sat quietly and prayed for yet one more miracle. Ten minutes later, the miracle came. The elevator doors opened. Sherry walked off. She was wearing a big grin on her face. "You can contact your nurses now," she said.

Amazed, Sister said, "I don't believe you!"

"Believe."

"What did you say to her?" asked Sister.

The manager replied, "I told Mrs. Clark that she would have to move out unless she agreed to let her daughter bring in a nurse."

Sister was astonished.

Jack said, "Nice job, Sherry."

Jack kissed his wife and went back to work. Sister went upstairs and visited with her mother.

"I guess these people won't give me any choice in the matter," Mo complained with a cough. She reached for a tissue and blew her nose. She threw the tissue on the floor.

"It looks that way, Momma," replied Sister as she picked up the tissue.

"Leave that alone," Mo coughed again. "Why don't you just run along now?" Another cough. She wiped her mouth with one more kleenex. It joined the others on the floor surrounding Mo's chair.

"If you want me to," Sister responded. "Do you need anything before I go? Are you thirsty?"

"For God's sake," she erupted. "I just want to watch my damn soaps."

Sister kissed her mother on the forehead. She turned back as she started to leave. Her mother had tears in her eyes. "Love you, Momma."

The corners of Mo's mouth turned up slightly.

The next day at 9:30 A.M., Sister met with the Hospice people in the lobby of Mo's building. Mary and Faith, the two women from Hospice, found Sister waiting in the conversation area. They wanted to go over what their program had to offer before they explained the details to her mother. After all Sister's questions were answered and the appropriate forms were completed and signed, the three of them went up to Mo's apartment.

Sister knocked on the door. There was no answer.

"Momma?"

Nothing.

"Momma?!" Sister couldn't budge the door. She left the two women standing there and raced downstairs for the security guard. He followed her back with a handful of keys. The man had a look of absolute panic on his face. Fumbling with the keys, he eventually managed to get her door unlocked. "Oh no," he muttered as the safety chain grabbed the door with a jerk.

Through the 4-inch crack, the two nurses, the guard, and her daughter could see the lifeless body of Mo Clark curled in a knot on the floor.

"Momma!" Sister yelled. "Momma, can you hear me?"

Mo moaned, "Hummmm?"

The guard ran for a cutting tool as the nurses watched helplessly over Sister's shoulder.

"Momma, it's all right," urged Sister, not believing her own hopeful words. Her eyes met those of the nurse and the lady in charge of the Hospice program. "Lord, help us. I am so glad you're both here."

"It won't be long now," assured one of the nurses. Even for professionals, they seemed to Sister to be most concerned. It was a horrifying few minutes. To Sister, as fast as the guard was running, he was moving in slow motion. Time was at a standstill, and she was powerless to speed things up. "I've got to get inside," she said over and over again. "I've got to see about Momma."

Finally, the guard reached the door. He snipped the chain and the four of them barged into Mo's apartment.

Mo tried to sit up. She looked like a tortured turtle rocking back and forth with its flippers helplessly flailing about.

"Wait, Mrs. Clark," said one of the nurses. "Let us see if you are hurt first."

Sister sat at her mother's feet trying to reassure her as the nurses checked her out.

At first very confused, Mo couldn't remember what had happened. "I don't know." She shook her head back and forth.

"Mrs. Clark, did you fall?" asked one nurse.

"I don't think so," she attempted to remember. Her eyes wild with fear. Who was this person asking questions?

"Momma, how long have you been on the floor?"

"The floor?" she puzzled. Sister looked at the Hospice women. Mo was obviously stunned.

"I should have known," Sister said to them. "I tried to call Momma earlier and got that busy signal. Of course," she explained, "That would be 'vintage Mo.' It would be just like

Momma to take the phone off the hook to avoid our coming over here today."

Instead, they figured out, Mo had knocked the telephone to the floor when she fell. And in falling, her mother also took with her the end table, a glass of water, a mound of papers, cigarettes and a full ashtray, the television schedule, and the "damn" TV clicker.

The nurse and Sister were able to get Mo up and into her chair.

"Who are you?" said her mother to Faith, the registered nurse.

Faith answered, "Mrs. Clark, I'm from Hospice. I came today because you said it was all right if I did."

"Oh, I suppose so," said Mo with a racking cough.

After a few minutes, Faith assured everyone in the room that her new patient hadn't broken anything and that she seemed to be none the worse after her fall. The security guard returned to his post. As Sister cleaned up the mess that fell from the table, the caregivers talked in detail about exactly what they would do for her.

Faith and Mary talked in hushed and gentle tones that conveyed concern. "We're here to be of help, Mrs. Clark," said Mary, "Everyone who works with us wants to make you as comfortable as we can."

At the end, Mo was subdued. Sister couldn't tell if her mother had listened to anything either of them said.

"Momma, I'm so relieved that you didn't get hurt," said Sister as she patted her mother's hand. "I am amazed at you. You have been great about this thing with the nurses."

"Good," replied Mo. "Now can I have my peace and quiet?" She then suggested as politely as she could, "All right, I agreed to let you come by on Monday, so now, let me be. Good-bye all." They left as told.

On Sunday, Sister was still shaken by Saturday's events. Again, she couldn't reach her mother by telephone. A busy signal droned on and on. Her whole body pounded in cadence with the sound.

Soon Jack and Sister were knocking on her mother's door. "Momma?"

Again nothing.

"Jack, what is this?!" said Sister alarmingly as she grabbed her husband's arm, "Poor Momma, I can't stand it."

He knocked forcefully. "Mo?"

Still no reply.

Sister ran for the guard, a different man, but had the same look in his eyes. His keys rattled. Ting, click, ting, jingle, click, and the door swung wide open. Mo was again on the floor in almost the very same spot. The phone was off the hook at her feet.

Sister knelt beside her. "Momma! You fell again."

Mo looked up at her daughter. That time she seemed even more disoriented. Her mother made no sound whatsoever.

"Momma, are you hurt?" Still no response. Jack and Sister carefully helped her to her chair. Her mind cleared a little. Mo said she thought she might have been there since everyone left on Saturday. Sister wanted to throw up.

She immediately called the Hospice number.

The Sanfords started around-the clock-nursing that same afternoon. Jack, as always, needed to do something to stay busy. "I'm going to clean up Mo's place," he announced. "We cannot let those people come into all this mess."

While Sister tidied up a little and tried to get her mother to drink something, Jack went to the store and came back with all manner of cleaning supplies. Later, dripping with sweat, disinfectant, and bleach, he came out of the bathroom. Jack proudly proclaimed, "Mo, I think we could do a bone marrow transplant in there!" He then tackled her kitchen. When they arrived at home later that night, Jack was completely exhausted. Nevertheless, he managed to remark, "I believe, after thirty years, your mother finally likes me."

Registered nurses, licensed practical nurses, and professional sitters started their rotations of caring for Mo. Sister was given the job of errand runner, clothes washer, and, most significantly, the job of *daughter*.

The week flew by. During that time, Sister met some of the other people in the building, people who actually knew Mo.

"How is Mo?" asked one neighbor.

"Not well at all. She has Hospice coming," Sister explained.

"Hospice, you say," the neighbor replied, probably knowing that Hospice usually implied the patient wouldn't be getting better. She added, "That's a shame, your mother is a lovely lady."

Sister was surprised to discover that Mo Clark had, for years, been faithful in sending many of her neighbors cards for Christmas and for their birthdays.

She mentioned finding out about that to her mother who was sitting in her chair watching television. Mo smiled slightly and said, "T'ain't nothin.'"

Sister found the man who lived next door to be a particularly compassionate soul. He asked Sister about her mother each and every day. One afternoon, the neighbor stopped Sister in the hall. "Got a minute?" he asked politely.

"Of course," she said. He gave her a note he had saved from her mother. The note read:

Please come over and turn on Channel 2 for me before you go out today.

Thanks. Mo Clark, Apt. 416.

Mo had found another way to work the remote control.

15

"I'm going to run downstairs and start the laundry, Momma," Sister called, arms managing the full bag. "I'll be back in a few minutes." Sister went down to the building's basement. Hauling her mother's bag full of linens and nighties, she went into the room where all the machines were. There was one whole wall of washers and another of dryers, a folding table, hanging racks, and several chairs. She had her wallet with her, but had no idea what it would cost. She had long been accustomed to the luxury of having her own machines at home. She condemned herself for not insisting that she do Mo's laundry all along.

The sign read, 60 CENTS PER LOAD. That was more than she had figured it would be. She had two huge loads. Sister opened her coin purse and found $1.20. It was exactly what she needed. "Perfect," she said.

"Oh, dear," she realized, "I forgot the detergent. How disorganized can one be?"

She noticed another lady who was doing her own laundry. Sister approached her pleadingly. "Do you have any detergent?" she asked.

The lady replied, "What? I'm sorry, I left my ear piece upstairs!"

Sister repeated loudly, "I just wondered if you had any soap?"

Only a quizzical look.

"Soap?" Sister shouted.

"Soap!" The lady smiled and nodded and gave Sister precisely two cupfuls of detergent.

"Thank you, you see, my mother is very sick," Sister tried to say loud enough to be heard.

"I left my ear piece upstairs," was her answer.

"Thank you," Sister said mouthing the words.

"I still can't hear you."

Sister stretched out her arms and embraced her laundry companion. The lady hugged her in response. For an unexplained reason, the both of them had tears in their eyes.

When Sister went back up to Mo's apartment, Rita, the LPN, said, "I found these quarters under Mrs. Clark's chair." She handed Sister the change. Sister counted the money. It was exactly enough to dry the two big loads of laundry.

Tuesday, a hospital bed was delivered. Her mother seemed more comfortable in it. However, as the delivery man was leaving, Mo pulled her daughter close to her and said emphatically, "Sister, stop that man. I want you to quit spending so damn much money!" When her daughter told her that the caregivers provided the bed for free, she was puzzled. "I don't believe a word of it," she said.

Wednesday, Sister asked a priest to come by and visit her mother. When Mo overheard the phone call, she coughed, "Who was that?" Sister told her it was Father Griffith. Mo erupted. With her rapidly failing voice, she croaked out the words, "No, no, no!"

Rita rose up from the chair by her patient's bed. Thus far, the nurse had gone about her business of quietly caring for Mo. Putting her hands on her ample hips, Rita raised her voice and commanded, "You go get that priest, baby! You go right this minute!"

Sister did exactly as she was told. She drove to the Sanford's church where Father Griffith was waiting in his car outside the office. A truly gentle person, Father Griffith was a recently ordained priest from Ireland. He waved sweetly to Sister and motioned for her to lead him to the apartment. Sister smiled and mouthed, "Thank you, Father."

As they entered the lobby, Sister placed a hand on Father Griffith's arm. "Momma used to be really involved in her religion," her voice trailed off. "Well, honestly, Father, she may be pretty hostile today," apologized Sister.

In his soft-spoken voice, the kind priest assured her, "I've seen just about everything, Sister. Please try not to worry."

As soon as they arrived, Rita made herself busy in the kitchen. Sister offered Father Griffith a chair. She took a seat at Mo's writing desk by the window. The young man pulled his chair closer to the dying lady. "Hello, Mrs. Clark, I'm Father Griffith from your daughter's parish."

"Hello," nodded Mo.

"Oh, would you look at this lovely porcelain doll. Is she yours, Mrs. Clark?"

"Yes," she acknowledged.

Sister added, "Momma calls her 'Party Doll.' She's had her since she was a little girl."

Mo's voice cracked. "And the bear, 'Teddy,'" she said with a cough.

"Ah, yes! I see. The fellow's had a hard time, it seems!" said the priest as he admired the two remaining treasures of Imogene Sinclair's childhood. She warmed somewhat to the sincere kindness of the priest.

Sister and Father Griffith prayed together the Lord's Prayer and the Hail Mary as Mo closed her eyes. Father read to her from his prayer book and then he anointed her with the oil of the sick. He stood over the dying woman and blessed her saying, "May God's peace comfort you and bless you, in the name of the Father and of the Son and of the Holy Spirit, Amen."

Mo's lips mouthed, "Amen."

Father Griffith quietly took his leave. Sister watched from her mother's window as he drove away.

On Friday afternoon, Mo pointed to her clock and gurgled in her pain-strained voice, "Sister, go home, it's traffic time."

Her daughter hesitated, "But, Momma."

"Traffic time," she fought to repeat.

"Okay, I'll go," she complied. Sister stroked her mother's hair. "Go to sleep, Momma. Remember, I love you."

Mo was eating crushed ice. It was the only thing she could still swallow. Sister and the caregivers fed her the tiny slivers from a silver spoon and a cup from her fine china. She hurried to finish the spoonful of ice, then swallowing hard, Mo said, "I love you, too."

Saturday morning, Sister stopped by the florist to get some flowers to cheer her mother. Holding an arrangement of peach colored roses, Sister spotted the two deep pink roses in a milk glass container. They were framed in baby's breath. She replaced her original selection and purchased the others. She then drove over to Mo's apartment.

"Good morning, Momma."

Mo was eating her ice and made no audible comment. To Sister, she seemed unusually agitated.

Martha, the LPN explained that Mrs. Clark had been very restless since she had come on duty early that morning.

Sister held the roses close to her mother's nose so she could smell them. "TaTa," Sister hoped she heard her mother saying. Just one more "*TaTa,*" *Momma,* she prayed quietly.

The day was long and short; it was tense and peaceful; it was incredibly sad. Mo ate ice and suffered. The nurse tended to her, and Sister fretted as she walked about the small apartment unable to do anything to ease her mother's pain. As the hours passed, Mo began to sleep fitfully. The nurse suggested that Sister go home and rest for awhile. She leaned over, kissed her mother's hair and said, "Night, night, Momma. I'll see you in a little bit."

Mo said, "Night, night."

Earlier in November, Sister had phoned her father in Florida to tell him that his ex-wife had been given only six months to live. His response had been a long, almost inaudible sigh. Harvey eventually gathered his thoughts and offered a very sincere, "I'm sorry, baby."

"It's okay, really, we're getting through it. Momma has cancer," she answered.

"I'm not surprised, she's smoked since she was twelve," he said. "Can I do anything to help you?"

"No, not that I can think of, Daddy," she said. "I appreciate that."

At first, Sister hadn't any intention of taking him up on his offer, but eventually, she began to reconsider her decision.

She knew full well that her father loved her. She realized that he felt guilty about leaving her with the sole responsibility of taking care of her mother. Harvey had once apologized saying that he hadn't expected that Mo would live for such a long time after their divorce.

Sister was aware of Harvey's mixed emotions regarding Mo and equally aware of the burden he carried. For all concerned, she decided it was a good idea to ask her father for his support.

In December, Sister called and said, "Daddy, do you still want to lend me a hand?"

"Of course I do. What do you have in mind?"

She explained, "Well, Daddy, there is one detail you could look into for me."

"What's that, honey?" he said.

"Please phone Memphis and get the number for Calvary Cemetery. Then call their business office and alert them that Imogene Sinclair Clark will be buried in the family plot, right next to Eugene Sinclair. My best guess is that it will take place sometime in the early spring," she said.

There was a pause. Then Harvey quickly said, "I'll be glad to. I'll call them today." Sister wondered what it was she had heard in his voice.

Her father didn't call for three days. When she answered her phone, she could tell from the sound of his voice that something was wrong. "I'm afraid I have some bad news for you. It seems that all thirteen graves in the Sinclair plot have been taken. Looks like they've messed us up, baby."

Sister held the phone, speechless.

"Baby," Harvey asked, "baby, are you okay?"

Sister ran her hand through her hair. "Let me give it some thought. Don't worry, I'll work something out."

"I'm sorry," he replied.

"It's okay, Daddy," she lied.

Sister told him good-bye and started to shake.

For as long as she could remember, all her mother ever really said she wanted was that one thing. She recalled as a child watching her mother go through the Whitman's Sampler box on Eugene Sinclair's birthday. Sometimes sober, more often drunk, Mo had always insisted, "Just bury me next to my Daddy."

Eliza, home for a visit, walked into the kitchen and found her mother crying. "Mom, what is it?"

"Oh," Sister replied, wiping her eyes, "the Sinclair plots, the grave plots in Memphis have all been taken. I can't bury Momma next to her father."

Eliza was silent for a moment.

"Mom," said Eliza, "why don't we cremate Grandma? Then we could bury her anywhere she wants."

Sister was appalled. "Eliza, *we* don't do that!"

"Why not?" she asked.

"We just don't," she decreed. Sister realized with a start that she was beginning to sound just like Mo.

Two weeks later, the cemetery in Memphis contacted Harvey. He relayed the message "Calvary decided they could make room for 'something smaller.'" Her father asked, "What the hell do you think that means?"

Sister replied, "You may not want to know the answer to that one, Daddy. I need to check out some things, and I'll call you back tomorrow." She was about to reach the conclusion that Eliza had made a good suggestion after all. Sister talked with several friends, with Father Griffith and with Jack, until, with some reservation, she reluctantly agreed on cremation. She realized it would be the only way to grant her mother her one last wish.

Jack went with Sister on her second trip to the funeral home. The two of them would replace the coffin, the one with the pink rose. That time they had to choose an urn.

The Sanfords arrived for their evening appointment. "Good evening," said the young man with whom they would make their decision. Soft and portly with a deep foreboding voice, he reminded Sister of a young Alfred Hitchcock.

"Good evening to you," she said, attempting to parrot his voice.

The mortician led Sister and Jack to the room where urns were displayed.

"This is so creepy," said Jack.

"You should have seen us the first time," remarked Sister. "You'll get used to the place soon."

If the coffin room had been bizarre, the urn room was twice so for Sister. She gazed around at the array of urns: some were bronze, others silver, still some were porcelain with flowers etched as decoration.

"Looks like we're in the mummy's tomb," said Sister in her Boris Karloff voice. Either she was trying to break her stress or she had gone over the edge.

Over the edge, assumed Jack as he put his arm around her.

She continued, "And here we are in Pharaoh's chamber. Look, his treasures are all about us."

"Just decide, Sister," he suggested.

"All right," she said.

She thought about her mother's collection of flower vases and realized that there would be no flowers displayed in the container they were going to purchase.

"Do you see anything you like?" the man asked.

Sister quickly decided on the bronze one. "That urn will do fine," she said, pointing to the one she liked the most.

"A very lovely choice," the man responded as if he were the waiter and she had just decided on the blackened salmon.

Jack noticed some very small urns on a lower shelf. He inquired, "What do you folks do with those little ones?" The oddly enthusiastic man explained that they were used when the deceased had a number of children who wanted to divvy up their parent, so to speak.

Hearing that, Jack and Sister nearly ran over each other as they made their way out of the display room. Jack excused their urgency and said, "Oh, thank you, but we'll only need one. My wife is an only child."

16

It was Saturday, January 17. Sister had been home for a couple of hours when the phone rang.

The voice asked for Mrs. Sanford.

"Yes, this is she."

The voice belonged to Joyce, Mo's LPN for the night. They had talked just an hour prior when she came for the evening shift. Mo liked Joyce.

"I was reading to Mrs. Clark from her prayer book," said Joyce. "I noticed a change in her. Mrs. Sanford, you'd best come at once. Your mother has taken a turn for the worse."

Sister was speechless. She gathered only her keys and hurried out the door.

Sister phoned her friend Jackie from the car. Jackie said that she and her husband were praying for Mo and for Sister. Sister kept talking with her friend as she drove down Peachtree Street. In a bizarre ritual, she chronicled every building, each traffic light, and her driving maneuvers. "I'm turning on to Piedmont Road," said Sister. "My stomach feels like it's in my throat."

"You'll be fine," coached Jackie. "God is there beside you."

"I know. I'm pulling into the parking lot. Jackie, I just looked up at Momma's window."

Until her last few days, Mo always stood in that window waving to Sister after each of their visits. Sometimes when she waved back to her mother or when she honked her horn as she drove away, Sister would think, *One of these days Momma won't be there.*

Sister stopped the car. Pulling on the emergency brake, she said, "I'm going inside now."

"God bless you," her friend whispered.

Joyce stood in the door. "I'm sorry. She's just passed," said the sympathetic woman.

Sister stood in the doorway, motionless, silent.

There was Momma. She was so tiny. Joyce had placed her blue crystal rosary in Mo's hands. Her hair was combed and she looked so calm. It was over.

Jack charged into the room just seconds behind his wife. "I'm sorry. I tried to catch up with you. The nurse called you back, but you'd already gotten to the end of our street," he panted.

He saw Mo's body and gasped, "Oh, my God."

Joyce recounted the details of what had happened. "I hung up from phoning you, Mrs. Sanford, then I turned back around to see my sweet Mrs. Clark. I said to her, 'Sister's on her way, dear. Would you like some ice?' Your mother never said another word."

Sister couldn't absorb what was going on. She noticed strange things. *How much like Grandee Momma looks in death*, she thought. *Suddenly, so old, so thin, so quiet.* Sister longed to believe what she really saw on her mother's face was peace.

"Are you doing all right?" asked Jack.

"I can't tell," Sister exhaled.

The next morning someone from the funeral home called. "Mrs. Sanford? Please come by at your convenience. You'll have to confirm that the body we have is that of Mrs. Imogene Clark."

"Of course," answered Sister

"It's just a formality," the man explained.

Sister asked Jack to go with her.

"Of course I will," he said.

"Thank you. I'm going to jump in the shower," Sister said.

When she got out, Jack told her that their children were on the way.

"I'm just not thinking at all, am I?" said Sister as she hugged her husband. "Thank you for calling them."

They went into the room where Mo's body had been placed for the viewing. Sister was again surprised. Her mother's hair had been combed exactly like Grandee's. The two could have been sisters.

She leaned close to her mother's face and spoke to her as if she were being heard. For a moment or two, they were back in Mo's apartment, drinking a Coke and chatting about everyday things. Mo was complaining about her soap opera being canceled because "some ridiculous politician was talking about something stupid."

"Momma, you were right about those politicians all along," she said absently.

Sister stroked her mother's forehead with only the tips of her fingers. She was afraid to feel the coolness of her skin. Sister said, "Momma, your hair looks so pretty. I had them put on your white dress, the one you wore to Edward's graduation."

"May I talk to you for a brief moment, Mrs. Sanford?" asked the director, touching her lightly on the elbow.

"Yes," she said. He motioned her downstairs. Jack was greeting Pam and her husband, David, so Sister reached out for William.

"Please," she said. That was all she had to say to the young man. Together they went into the man's office.

He apologetically began, "I am required to ask you just one quick question."

What on earth? Sister thought. "Of course," she said.

"Would you like for us to give you your mother's prosthetic hip?" he asked.

"*What* did you say?" screamed Sister.

William's mouth was agape, his eyes looked like they were on springs.

The director repeated, shakily, "Your mother's prosthetic hip, do you want it?"

"Momma's hip?" questioned Sister in disbelief. At that point, having completely lost her sense of propriety, Mo's daughter reached across the table and grabbed the funeral director's hands.

"What in the world would I do with my mother's hip?" she asked. "Turn it into a lamp?"

The shaken man slowly peeled himself from her grasp, patted her hand, and explained that sometimes people like to keep things like that. "You would be surprised, Mrs. Sanford. Why, only the last week, we had a client who wanted to see how well his mother's prosthesis had held up. It seemed that he had one of his own and wanted to see how long he could expect his to last."

"No, we're all still in one piece. That won't be necessary," she stammered.

Earlier on the phone, Sister's friend Ave had asked if she could bring anything special to the funeral home.

"How about your tape player? Maybe we could use some music," Sister answered her friend.

During their brief conversation, Sister had pictured Jack and herself, along with their children, Pam, Jackie and Ave. She imagined the small group standing together near her mother.

"Yes," Ave agreed, "I think some music might ease the moment."

Then, on a whim Sister added, "Ave, do you think you could find something we might have sung when we were little girls in a May procession?"

"I'll do my best," she promised.

Sister stood before Mo's body for just a few more minutes. "You're not really there, are you? Are you already in Heaven?" she mused. "Momma, are you watching us right now?" Sister's mind was jumping in ten directions and she wasn't aware of the movement going on behind her. As she turned around, she was amazed to find a room of friends smiling kindly.

In one short hour, the ladies had gathered a group of caring people to honor Mo. A circle formed and joined hands with Sister, Jack, and the children.

"Thank you all for coming," Sister smiled. "I can't tell you how surprised I am and, even more, how very much your being here means to me." In an irreverent, and very genuine moment, she admitted, "I must say to you, however, Momma would be ill at ease about this. She's very shy, you may know."

Turning to her mother, Sister said, "Everyone, this is Momma. This is Sarah Imogene Sinclair Clark. This is Mo."

Sister paused briefly and said, "Momma, these are my friends."

There were soft responses from the circle.

Sister concluded, "My mother knows about a good many of you. She always listens when I tell her stories about my friends."

The circle laughed quietly.

Ave turned on the music. Sister explained to the group that what they were going to experience was a "Catholic thing." "When I was a little girl growing up in Memphis, our school, St. Agnes Academy had annual May processions. They were usually planned to be on Mother's Day," Sister began. "We all wore our Easter dresses and marched two by two as we sung hymns honoring the Blessed Mother. We had flowers in our hair. Momma always made my headpiece from the roses that grew in our backyard."

Ave turned on her music.

"On this day, oh beautiful mother, on this day, we give you our love." Tears streamed down Sister's face as she sang with Ave. Jack hurried over to her with a tissue. She wiped her eyes. Eliza was crying softly. Edward walked to another room to get a cup of cold water. The circle swayed back and forth as the participants stumbled through trying to sing three verses of the May hymn.

As she stood there, Sister thought about the deep pink roses that she positioned under her mother's nose for her to smell. Had that been just yesterday? Only thirty hours ago, was it? Now as her mother lay in her coffin she held those same roses in her cold, waxen hands.

Ave turned on her second selection. Sister's eyes opened wide and a smile split her face as a hymn sung by Elvis Presley filled the room. She said, "Ave, my mother absolutely despised Elvis! Momma always said 'Elvis Presley is nothing but poor white trash.' But my Grandee thought his music was spiritual in the truest sense of the word."

The circle laughed heartily.

For the next week, Sister rode a roller coaster of emotion. Her tears were punctuated with laughter. One minute, she needed absolute quiet; another, she craved thunderous classical music abounding with drums and cymbals. She couldn't manage to eat more than a couple of bites of dinner, then only minutes later, she'd dive in and consume an entire box of wheat crackers. She needed the company of people, and she needed to be totally alone. Her singular constant demand was for light; sunshine in the day, every lamp lit at night. Sister couldn't abide the darkness.

Every morning that week, she attended Mass. On one of those mornings, she turned around to extend her hand in the Sign of Peace. Much to her surprise, she found a nun with her own hand reaching toward her. The kind faced sister was dressed in the traditional habit of the Sisters of St. Dominic. "And peace be with you, my dear," she said sweetly. A gift from Momma and from Grandee, Sister believed.

After Mass, she drove to Mo's apartment. She usually picked up a donut along the way. Lemon filled. Lunch, if she felt like eating, was always a cheeseburger. Her diet, generally leaning toward low fat, completely changed during her mother's warp-speed illness and sudden death.

Sister gazed around Mo's apartment. She took the seat she had never before occupied. It was Mo's chair. She could feel the indention of her mother's cancer-shrunken body. She again marveled at her mother's courage.

"Momma, you treated throat cancer with aspirin and cough drops," said Sister, shaking her head in wonder. Half expecting her mother to answer, she asked, "Why wouldn't you take the pain medication the doctor sent and the Hospice nurses pleaded with you to take? Did the spoonfuls of crushed ice help at all?" Familiar tears welled up in Sister's eyes.

Next to her was the sadly vacant hospital bed. Her memory of the night her mother died included an image. What was it? She dismissed the thought.

"Just pick the bed up, please pick it up as soon as you can!" she had begged the young woman at the supply company who answered the telephone. How many times had Mo held that same phone and talked with her?

Mo's neighbors dropped in throughout the day while Sister was going through the apartment. "Momma finally did make friends, after all," she again noted. The thoughtful man next door, the one who had helped her mother with Jack's television, gave Sister a photo copy of the Christmas note Mo had slipped under his door. She had struggled to scribble the words, *Thanks for all the help with the TV. Happy Birthday on December 23.*

The neighbor remarked, "I hope you won't mind having a copy, I'd like to keep the original for myself."

"Of course not," she said, looking fondly at the note. "I'm just pleased to have it."

The lady at the front desk told Sister about receiving a similar note. She mentioned that Mrs. Clark had written a dozen or more people in the apartment building. In talking with the residents and in looking through the nooks and crannies of Mo's place, she was discovering what her mother regarded as her life's treasures. Sister was just beginning to comprehend the tremendous strives her mother had made.

Wednesday, Sister was in her car in the donut store drive-thru when she took time to check her phone messages.

"You have one message" it said.

The lady handed her the sack with coffee and a cinnamon twist.

"Thank you," she said as she pressed "1" to hear the message.

"Mrs. Sanford, your mother's 'cremains' are ready to be picked up," announced the voice who identified himself as being from the funeral home.

She drove to Mo's apartment and pitched her breakfast in the trash.

It was Friday at 4:45 P.M. and Sister knew she'd be flying to Memphis early the next morning. She drove into the parking lot of the funeral home. *Odd,* she thought, *it seems there are generally a good many cars here.* Sister pulled into a spot. Going to the front door, she attempted to turn the knob. It was locked. She knocked. She rang the bell. Anxiety rising, Sister ran around to the back of the building. No success. Running back to her car, Sister grabbed the phone. 411. "Yes, please, I need the telephone number."

"Which location?" asked the voice.

Sister was standing under the sign. She read off the address.

The answering service picked up. Sister's voice, at an unusually high pitch, squealed, "Help, I'm in your parking lot. My mother, Imogene Clark, is trapped inside the building! I'm supposed to fly to Memphis early tomorrow. I must have Momma, it's her funeral!"

Within a few minutes, three men came to the front door and motioned to the hysterical woman. One held open the door and told her, "We were working downstairs." The trio was uniformly dressed in black pants and white shirts and all had their sleeves rolled up.

The spokesman for the trio said he had received the page from their service. "I'm glad we were still here," he said, smiling graciously at Sister.

"Me, too," she breathed.

He gestured toward an ornate ebony desk. On it was an urn, bronze. Momma.

A second one of the men brushed his pants. Sister noticed what appeared to be ashes. Staring at the gray sprinkles, she inquired, "Is that my mother?"

"No, ma'am, of course not," he replied. The third man quickly suggested that he would be happy to put Mrs. Clark's cremains in a box for Mrs. Sanford. Gratefully, she nodded to the affirmative. She couldn't take her eyes off the urn or off the ashes that still remained on the other fellow's trousers.

She remembered to clarify a couple of concerns about boarding the airplane with the urn. Would she need a permit? They answered her questions and also provided her with the appropriate documents so she could easily get through the airport without any problem. The spokesman then offered to carry the box and its contents to her car.

"Yes, thank you," Sister said.

Sister opened the car door and the man leaned in with the box. He started to put it on floor.

"Wait!" Sister shouted. "My mother cannot ride on the floor!" He carefully placed Mo on the seat. Sister reached for the seatbelt and buckled it. "Momma steadfastly refused to wear a seatbelt. This time I will insist she does."

Before Sister could thank the young man, he scooted away from her and retreated into the saner confines of the funeral parlor.

A few minutes later, she was at the dry cleaners. "Oh yes, of course, your coat is ready to go. You have several other items, as well," said Nick, the owner. "I'll put them in your car for you."

Sister thought about the urn. "*No!*" she said. "I mean, no thank you, Nick. I'll just take it all myself." She paid for the dry cleaning, gathered her things, and loaded the clothes into the back seat.

Everyone was dragging along caught in the bumper to bumper Friday traffic muddle. "Momma, I am sorry about that stop at the cleaners. I know how you hate running errands."

A red light flashed bright on the dashboard. "*Check your fuel gauge,*" it said.

Great, just great, thought Sister.

"Momma, some things never change. I hope you're laughing." She could almost envision her mother's smirk. Momma would shake her head and say, "What did I do to deserve my little i'jit?"

She turned into a service station to get some gas.

The owner was at the counter when she went inside to pay. Always a courteous person, Chuck Allen and his family had owned the neighborhood station for as long as anyone could remember. He inquired about her family.

"Oh yes, thank you, Chuck. They're all doing fine."

"Good to hear," smiled Chuck as Sister signed her ticket.

"Thanks again," she nodded her head. Sister came very close to saying, "You know what? I do have Momma in the car."

Then she thought better of it.

She drove directly home, making no more stops. She parked in the garage and unlocked the back door. Sister unloaded the cleaning and put her purse on the kitchen counter top. Retrieving the urn from the front seat, she gingerly carried it through the same door her mother had walked so many times.

Sister placed the urn on the buffet next to the white Victorian basket, the one that her mother had given her for Christmas. Her eyes were fixed on the little cherub. Blond hair with blue eyes just like Mo. *My God,* Sister thought. *Momma's body had been incinerated.*

Sister stood in front of the make-shift altar and stared at the urn.

17

The white monuments glistened in the sun's light. For a January morning in Memphis, it was not too terribly cold unless the wind gusted. Sister stood gazing at Calvary Cemetery. Her family milled behind her, speaking in low tones. She turned at the sound of approaching footsteps.

"Hello baby!" It was her father. She hurried to greet him.

"Oh, I'm so glad to see you!" she cried as she hugged him tightly.

"You knew I'd be here," he said.

"I suppose I did." She smiled.

He greeted William with a handshake.

"It's good to see you, Papaw," William said.

Just then other family friends and relatives began to show up. Sister was delighted. "Daddy, you made some calls, didn't you?"

Her father grinned saying he was just glad there was something he could do.

As Harvey and William chatted, Sister caught sight of the Harrisons, Mary Catherine, who had been Mo's lifelong friend, and her husband Ed. They got out of their car and came over toward Sister. "I am deeply sorry about your mother," said Mary Catherine. "We had no idea she was so ill."

Sister briefly told the story of the last few days of Mo's life. "I was so proud of her. She really was so courageous, Mrs. Harrison. Did you know that she treated the cancer with just Bayer's aspirin and Mentholatum?"

Mary Catherine laughed a little. "That's just like her. Bless her soul."

Sister nodded.

They embraced.

"I do have something of a surprise for you," said Mary Catherine.

Her surprise was the appearance of Margaret Harrison: the Margaret of the talent shows, the Margaret of the forts and playhouses and bike rides. The two childhood playmates hadn't seen each other for thirty years. When Margaret stepped out from the back seat of the Harrisons' car, Sister put her hands to her mouth mutely. She ran into her old friend's arms. "Margaret!"

"Sister!" They held each other and cried and rocked back and forth. Margaret was carrying a single yellow rose. She blinked back her own tears and said, "I remember, your mother used to fix us such wonderful lunches. She trimmed the crust off the sandwiches and put potato chips and olives on the side for us. I brought this to your mother because she always grew those beautiful roses in the brick garden."

A van full of flowers wouldn't have thrilled Sister more.

The priest arrived apologizing for being somewhat late. To which Sister replied, "Your timing couldn't have been better, Father."

Everyone got into their automobiles and drove in a slow procession through the winding paths of Calvary Cemetery. Sister looked out the car window as she passed so many familiar Memphis names chiseled in marble and granite.

At the graveside service, the priest spoke of peace. He didn't know Mo except for one phone conversation with her daughter just two days earlier, yet he was able to say appropriate things about healing and forgiveness. For her part, Sister was to read Psalm 23. In fact, she had practiced doing so. The copy she wanted to use was typed in 1963 by Grandee as she sat at her desk at the Ellis Auditorium.

At the bottom of the page, Grandee had written in pencil, *Peace I leave with you. My peace I give unto you not as the world giveth, give I unto you. Let not your heart be troubled, neither let it be afraid.*

Sister stood before the small group of mourners who had gathered to honor her mother. She read Psalm 23 flawlessly. Yet, standing at the foot of her grandparents' graves, getting ready to watch as her mother's remains were added to theirs, Sister touched her finger to Grandee's own handwriting. She got as far as "*Peace I leave with you...,*" and she stopped. She couldn't read another word.

William hurried to his mother's side. He continued, "My peace I give unto you not as the world giveth give I unto you. Let not your heart be troubled, neither let it be afraid."

The Sinclair plot was then complete. There were fourteen of them all there together. Among them were precious Grandee and her Eugene. Mo's cousin Howard. Will and his wife Ann. And on that day, January 24, 1998, Sarah Imogene Sinclair Clark joined the rest of her family.

"Peace be with you all and with you, Momma," said Sister as she placed Margaret's yellow rose by her mother's urn.

18

The following week, Sister continued the task of cleaning out her mother's apartment. She found an antique silver flask, tarnished into gold after decades without use; it bore the initials E.W.S. Sister found a yellowed newspaper clipping, the death announcement of Eugene Sinclair. It was then she discovered the shocking coincidence. Her wedding rehearsal and his death shared the same day, June 23.

> SINCLAIR—Suddenly, at residence, 1893 Harbert Ave., Thursday, June 23, 1932, at 4:25 o'clock. Eugene W. Sinclair, aged 43 years, husband of Mrs. Sarah N. Sinclair, father of Miss Sarah Imogene Sinclair. Son of the late Mr. and Mrs. William E. Sinclair. Brother of Mr. William G. Sinclair. Services, conducted by the Rev. D. J. Murphy, will be held at the parlors of McDowell & Monteverde, 531 Vance Ave. Friends invited Friday afternoon at 3 o'clock. Internment private at Calvary Cemetery.

"Momma, Grandee, I am so very sorry," Sister said. Her eyes shut, her hands cupping her face. "So terribly, terribly sorry."

Sister found correspondence from Mo's friends of long ago. The cards and letters were tied neatly with faded ribbons. Sister found birthday and Christmas cards from her mother's new acquaintances who lived in the building. With the cards, she found a spiral-bound notebook with a detailed list of names, apartment numbers, and dates of birth.

"Momma, you put so much effort into remembering people's birthdays," Sister said as if Mo were listening. "Good for you."

Sister found her own grade school report cards: almost all A's; she never remembered doing that well. Looking at her third grade report, she thought about all the blue birds and stars that Sisters Pelegia and Georgejeanne Marie had awarded her. There wasn't the first blue bird in Mo's keepsakes. Nevertheless, her mother had been a good bit more aware of her accomplishments than she'd realized.

She found her own self-portrait from third grade that she had fashioned into a Christmas card for her mother. On it, Sister had carefully drawn her green eyes and freckles, and chestnut brown hair combed into a pageboy. Oh, and, of course, very predominantly illustrated were angel's wings.

She found newspaper clippings of the Sanford family that Mo had saved. She reread her own engagement announcement. It took her back to the day she posed for that picture in the studio. "Think about your boyfriend," the photographer coached her. She remembered laughing. And there was their wedding write-up. "Jack and I look like children!" she thought to her amazement. "Lord, I thought we were so awfully grown up."

Sister gathered the items that seemed most significant to Mo and to herself and carefully put them into bags and boxes. Load by load, she took her mother's things to the car.

Lastly, she picked up Mo's bedraggled "Teddy" and her porcelain "Party Doll" that Father Griffith had so admired when he visited. Carrying the bear and the doll as carefully as she would two small children, Sister gingerly placed them on the front seat and drove home.

Sister and Jack took one evening and went over to pick up what they hadn't already given away. Lifting, pushing, pulling and dragging, they managed to move a few chosen pieces of Mo's furniture to the freight elevator, onto the loading dock, and into a borrowed truck. They took Grandee's dresser, the one with the special treats drawer, and the marble top desk where Mo had written all her letters. The new television with the remote was, of course, set aside for William, and Mo's bedroom furniture was what Eliza had requested. A few other items were to be stored in the Sanford's basement.

"Whew, I'm tired," admitted Jack. He was understandably exhausted. After all, the man had done the majority of the heavy lifting.

"Of course you are, Jack. Why don't you go on home? We'll get the boys and unload everything over the weekend," suggested Sister. "I'd like to hang around here for a couple of minutes," she said. "I'll be home after a while." She hugged her husband. He went down to the truck and she watched as he drove off.

Sister stood in Mo's living room. She could close her eyes and see everything back in its place. There was her mother sitting in her chair watching television, drinking a Coke, a cigarette perched on her fingertips. She went into the empty bedroom and remembered her mother's last night in there, the uncomfortably miserable night before the hospital bed was delivered and placed in the middle of the living room. She could still envision the nurse holding on to her suffering patient as the two made the few agonizing steps so she could have a bath. It had been Mo's last.

She made one final check of all the closets, the cabinets, and behind the doors. Sister reached for her cell phone to call Jack and say she was on her way. She dialed her mother's number by mistake? Not really, she wanted to hear her mother's sober voice one last time. The cruel machine refused her permission. "The number you are calling has been disconnected."

Sister looked out from Mo's window. It was getting late. The moon had gone behind a cloud and only the street light shined on her car. She took a quick glance, locked the door of the apartment, and took her mother's keys downstairs. She carried the shopping cart and her purse. Mo's keys jingled in her pocket.

In the daytime, the lobby was a beehive of chatting residents. At that hour, the hive was as silent as a tomb. Sister felt all the more alone as she looked at the vacant chairs. The accommodating ladies at the desk had long since gone home when she placed the keys where they'd be easily spotted in the morning. Sister was feeling completely empty, just as if she were the old, yellow-brick building with its silent halls, sleeping inhabitants, and unoccupied desk.

In her obsession to put things in order, Sister went into a frenzy of cleaning and organizing her own home. In doing so, Sister had recovered from an old trunk a picture of Mo as a child. Sister picked up a picture of her mother that had sat on Grandee's dresser as long as she could remember. In the photograph, the adorable five-year-old Imogene is dressed in an ermine coat and bonnet and carries a matching muff. She wears high-top button shoes. Her blond curls frame her face as her little blue eyes squint in the sunshine.

"It's long past time you had a bath." Sister was clearly talking to herself again. She recognized that. "I'll bet that the glass on your frame hasn't been shined properly in thirty years."

Sister popped off the back of the frame and carefully eased the photograph of Imogene out from its antique wooden walls. Revealed behind the picture was something Sister had never seen and had not the slightest idea even existed. "Well, hello, and you must be Sarah Sinclair!" she exclaimed.

Like a treasure chest, the old walnut frame had safeguarded the photograph of her grandmother taken, Sister guessed, when Grandee was somewhere in her forties. It was a picture of Grandee before she was Grandee. Dressed as a professional, she is wearing a handsome felt hat, a black suit and a white blouse with starched white collar and cuffs. Her hands are folded as her face turns to look directly into the camera. Sarah's mouth is gently closed as her dimples reveal a sweet, soft, yet strong and confident smile.

Sister laid the two photographs, Sarah and Imogene, side by side and studied them silently. Slowly, a smile crept over Sister's face.

19

"Warm for February," Sister said to herself some weeks later as she started out to take Nestle for a walk. The sun cheered the gray winter sky. Some of the more courageous green daffodil shoots had broken through the pine straw on the path that ran beside the Sanfords' driveway. As she put the leash on her dog, a bright red cardinal flew in front of them and perched on the dogwood tree in the yard next door.

Sister paused to watch the bird preen herself, thinking back to something she'd glimpsed at the foot of Mo's deathbed, an indistinct figure. "What do you think, Nestle, was it a ghost?" she asked.

The dog stopped to sniff her neighbor's recycle bin.

"That's no answer," laughed Sister.

As soon as they returned from the walk, Sister resolved herself to call Mary, who had been the coordinator for Mo's care.

"I don't know how weird this is going to sound," Sister began, "but I must tell you something." As the words started from her lips, like Jack, she questioned her mental state. "Mary, I think I saw, or *might* have seen—Mary, I can't explain this very well."

"Are you going to be home this afternoon?" asked the coordinator.

"Yes, but why?"

"I'd like to drop by," she explained.

"Of course, please come. Come any time. I'll be here."

Later that afternoon, Sister greeted Mary warmly at the door. "I almost regret bothering you with this. I'm pretty much embarrassed," said Sister as the two women made their way to the kitchen.

"This is what we do. I'm here to help," Mary replied. "Do you feel like talking?"

The two women sat in the kitchen as Sister started a fresh pot of coffee. It made her more comfortable to be doing something with her hands.

"It's just that I believe I saw—" Again she hesitated. The coffee perked in the background.

"I know what you saw," said Mary softly. "I saw him, too."

"What?! Him! You saw the man?" gasped Sister. Cups clattered as she took them from the cabinet. Sister tried to pour cream into a pitcher; she spilled it on the counter top.

Mary nodded. "We were waiting for the ambulance to come for your mother's body. I was at the far end of the room with Mrs. Clark's nurse. I remember that you were sitting near the hospital bed. You were talking on the telephone."

"Daddy! Yes, I was talking to my father. He was extremely upset. I was surprised at his reaction. In fact, so much so that I almost believed it was Daddy I saw!" She began to shake as a chill ran up her back and radiated into her arms and legs. She poured the two cups of coffee and sat down across from Mary.

"The image I saw stood at the foot of Mrs. Clark's bed gazing at her."

"Yes!" Sister exclaimed. She put the cup back on its saucer. Her hands trembled.

Mary said, "It seems like he was extending his hand toward her, but I can't be sure."

"Oh, my God," said Sister. "It happened so fast. I was almost too afraid to let myself see him, whatever he was. It was as if I blinked and he disappeared." Sister quieted. Then she asked, " Mary! Was this an angel?"

Mary replied, "Or someone who has been very special to your mother. Someone who had come to escort her."

Sister whispered, "Eugene Sinclair."

"Who?" asked Mary.

"He was very special to Momma," Sister replied. "Eugene was her father who died when she was eighteen years old. She missed him for the rest of her life."

"She's with him now," remarked Mary.

"And with Grandee," beamed Sister.

"Your grandfather must have died fairly young, I assume," commented Mary. "What happened to him?"

Sister looked into her coffee cup a moment. "After a tragic automobile accident, he took his own life," she said firmly.

Mary shook her head in disbelief. "That had to be so hard for your mother. Were you and she close?"

Sister grinned into her coffee cup.

"Very."